Drive

JAMES SALLIS

Drive

A HARVEST BOOK
HARCOURT, INC.
Orlando   Austin   New York   San Diego   Toronto   London

www.HarcourtBooks.com

First published by Poisoned Pen Press in 2005

Library of Congress Cataloging-in-Publication Data
Sallis, James, 1944-
Drive/James Sallis.—1st Harvest ed.
p.   cm.
1. Stunt performers—Fiction.   2.Stunt driving—Fiction.
3.Criminals—Fiction.   I. Title.
PS3569.A462D75   2006
813'.54—dc22   2006014788
ISBN-13: 978-0-15-603032-8

Text set in Adobe Garamond

Printed in the United States of America

First Harvest edition 2006
E G I K J H F D

PRAISE FOR Drive

"Full throttle . . . Sallis's riveting novella reads the way a Tarantino or Soderbergh neo-noir plays, artfully weaving through Driver's haunted memory and fueled by confident storytelling and keen observations about moviemaking, low-life living, and, yes, driving. Short and not so sweet, *Drive* is one lean, mean, masterful machine. Grade: **A**."   —*Entertainment Weekly*

"Sallis has written a perfect piece of noir fiction. In telling the good-man-gone-bad story of a Hollywood stunt driver named, appropriately enough, Driver, this master stylist uses a cinematic idiom of jump-cut, nonsequential scenes to focus on those hollowed-out moments when a man's moral landscape suddenly shifts

"*Drive*
lence,
life. T
with ;

"Sallis has combined the plot of a pulp novel from the '40s with the atmosphere of a French film noir into one stark and stunning tale of murder, treachery, and deceit . . . [*Drive*] packs a wallop that far outweighs its page count . . . For those who have not yet had the chance to read one of crime fiction's most underappreciated writers, now is the perfect opportunity." —*The Boston Globe*

"Imagine the heart of Jim Thompson beating in the poetic chest of James Sallis and you'll have some idea of the beauty, sadness and power of *Drive* . . . [It] has more thought, feeling and murderous energy than books twice its length."   —*Chicago Tribune*

"Refreshing, even startling . . . a lovely piece of work that makes you wish some other writers would take lessons from [Sallis]."
— *The Washington Post Book World*

"The slim novel underscores what power this author commands with spare, gem-like prose, brisk action and a Camus-like hero."
— *Sun-Sentinel* (Fort Lauderdale)

"A beautifully controlled, lean but far from skeletal literary gem . . . totally original."
— *OC Metro*

"This is just about as perfect a specimen of short crime fiction as you are likely to find. In fact, there's crime fiction that aspires to literature. And then, once in a great while, there's literature that just happens to be crime fiction. Cut and polished to a mirror-like luster, the latter is what you get with the little gem that is *Drive*."
— James Clar, *The Mean Streets*

"Sallis has a bloodhound's nose for noir . . . Sometimes [his characters] know they're trapped, and sometimes they are the last ones to know, but Sallis always knows; he can smell it in their pores, and he makes us smell it, too . . . in one crisply written spot-on scene after another . . . in this hypnotic little story about driving circles around your life."
— *Booklist* (starred review)

"In this masterfully convoluted neo-noir . . . Sallis gives us his most tightly written mystery to date, worthy of comparison to the compact, exciting oeuvre of French noir giant Jean-Patrick Manchette."
— *Publishers Weekly* (starred review)

"Noir at its pulpiest best."
— *Library Journal*

To Ed McBain,
Donald Westlake and
Larry Block—
three great American writers

Drive

Chapter One

Much later, as he sat with his back against an inside wall of a Motel 6 just north of Phoenix, watching the pool of blood lap toward him, Driver would wonder whether he had made a terrible mistake. Later still, of course, there'd be no doubt. But for now Driver is, as they say, in the moment. And the moment includes this blood lapping toward him, the pressure of dawn's late light at windows and door, traffic sounds from the interstate nearby, the sound of someone weeping in the next room.

The blood was coming from the woman, the one who called herself Blanche and claimed to be from New Orleans even when everything about her except the put-on accent screamed East Coast—Bensonhurst, maybe, or some other far reach of Brooklyn. Blanche's shoulders lay across the bathroom door's threshhold. Not much of her head left in there: he knew that.

Their room was 212, second floor, foundation and floors close enough to plumb that the pool of blood advanced slowly, tracing the contour of her body just as he had, moving toward him like an accusing finger. His arm hurt like a son of a bitch. This was the other thing he knew: it would be hurting a hell of a lot more soon.

Driver realized then that he was holding his breath. Listening for sirens, for the sound of people gathering on stairways or down in the parking lot, for the scramble of feet beyond the door.

Once again Driver's eyes swept the room. Near the half-open front door a body lay, that of a skinny, tallish man, possibly an albino. Oddly, not much blood there. Maybe blood was only waiting. Maybe when they lifted him, turned him, it would all come pouring out at once. But for now, only the dull flash of neon and headlights off pale skin.

The second body was in the bathroom, lodged securely in the window from outside. That's where Driver had found him, unable to move forward or back. This one had carried a shotgun. Blood from his neck had gathered in the sink below, a thick pudding. Driver used a straight razor when he shaved. It had been his father's. Whenever he moved into a new room, he set out his things first. The razor had been there by the sink, lined up with toothbrush and comb.

Just the two so far. From the first, the guy jammed in the window, he'd taken the shotgun that felled the second. It was a Remington 870, barrel cut down to the length of the magazine, fifteen inches maybe. He knew that from a *Mad Max* rip-off he'd worked on. Driver paid attention.

Now he waited. Listening. For the sound of feet, sirens, slammed doors.

What he heard was the drip of the tub's faucet in the bathroom. That woman weeping still in the next room. Then something else as well. Something scratching, scrabbling....

Some time passed before he realized it was his own arm jumping involuntarily, knuckles rapping on the floor, fingers scratching and thumping as the hand contracted.

Then the sounds stopped. No feeling at all left in the arm, no movement. It hung there, apart from him, unconnected, like an abandoned shoe. Driver willed it to move. Nothing happened.

Worry about that later.

He looked back at the open door. Maybe that's it, Driver thought. Maybe no one else is coming, maybe it's over. Maybe, for now, three bodies are enough.

Chapter Two

Driver wasn't much of a reader. Wasn't much of a movie person either, you came right down to it. He'd liked *Road House*, but that was a long time back. He never went to see movies he drove for, but sometimes, after hanging out with screenwriters, who tended to be the other guys on the set with nothing much to do for most of the day, he'd read the books they were based on. Don't ask him why.

This was one of those Irish novels where people have horrible knockdowndragouts with their fathers, ride around on bicycles a lot, and occasionally blow something up. Its author peered out squinting from the photograph on the inside back cover like some life form newly dredged into sunlight. Driver found the book in a secondhand store out on Pico, wondering whether the old-lady proprietor's sweater or the books smelled mustier. Or maybe it was the old lady herself.

Old people had that smell about them sometimes. He'd paid his dollar-ten and left.

Not that he could tell the movie had anything to do with this book.

Driver'd had some killer sequences in the movie once the hero smuggled himself out of north Ireland to the new world (that was the book's title, *Sean's New World*), bringing a few hundred years' anger and grievance with him. In the book, Sean came to Boston. The movie people changed it to L.A. What the hell. Better streets. And you didn't have to worry so much about weather.

Sipping at his carryout horchata, Driver glanced up at the TV, where fast-talking Jim Rockford did his usual verbal prance-and-dance. He looked back down, read a few more lines till he fetched up on the word *desuetude*. What the hell kind of word was that? He closed the book and put it on the nightstand. There it joined others by Richard Stark, George Pelecanos, John Shannon, Gary Phillips, all of them from that same store on Pico where hour after hour ladies of every age arrived with armloads of romance and mystery novels they swapped two for one.

Desuetude.

At the Denny's two blocks away, Driver dropped coins in the phone and dialed Manny Gilden's number, watching people come and go in the restaurant. It was a popular spot, lots of families, lots of people if they sat down by you you'd be inclined to move over a notch or two, in a neighborhood where slogans on T-shirts and greeting cards at the local Walgreen's were likely to be in Spanish.

Maybe he'd have breakfast after, it was something to do.

He and Manny had met on the set of a science fiction movie in which, in one of many post-apocalypse Americas, Driver had command of an El Dorado outfitted to look like a tank. Wasn't a hell of a lot of difference in the first place, to his thinking, between a tank and that El Dorado. They handled about the same.

Manny was one of the hottest writers in Hollywood. People said he had millions tucked away. Maybe he did, who knew? But he still lived in a run-down bungalow out towards Santa Monica, still wore T-shirts and chinos with chewed-up cuffs over which, on formal occasions such as one of Hollywood's much-beloved meetings, an ancient corduroy sports coat worn virtually cordless might appear. And he was from the streets. No background to amount to anything, no degree. Once when they were having a quick drink, Driver's agent told him that Hollywood was composed almost entirely of C+ students from Ivy League universities. Manny, who got pulled in for everything from script-doctoring Henry James adaptations to churning out quickie scripts for genre films like *Billy's Tank*, kind of put the lie to that.

His machine picked up, as always.

*You know who this is or you wouldn't be calling.
With any luck at all, I'm working. If I'm not— and
if you have money for me, or an assignment—please
leave a number. If you don't, don't bother me, just
go away.*

"Manny," Driver said. "You there?"

"Yeah. Yeah, I'm here….Hang a minute?…I'm right at the end of something."

"You're always at the end of something."

"Just let me save….There. Done. Something radically new, the producer tells me. Think Virginia Woolf with dead bodies and car chases, she says."

"And you said?"

"After shuddering? What I always say. Treatment, redo, or a shooting script? When do you need it? What's it pay? Shit. Hold on a minute?"

"Sure."

"…Now *there's* a sign of the times. Door-to-door natural-foods salesmen. Like when they used to knock on your door with half a cow butchered and frozen, give you a great deal. So many steaks, so many ribs, so much ground."

"Great deals are what America's all about. Had a woman show up here last week pitching tapes of whale songs."

"What'd she look like?"

"Late thirties. Jeans with the waistband cut off, faded blue workshirt. Latina. It was like seven in the morning."

"I think she swung by here, too. Didn't answer, but I looked out. Make a good story—if I wrote stories anymore. What'd you need?"

"Desuetude."

"Reading again, are we? Could be dangerous....It means to become unaccustomed to. As in something gets discontinued, falls into disuse."

"Thanks, man."

"That it?"

"Yeah, but we should grab a drink sometime."

"Absolutely. I've got *this* thing, which is pretty much done, then a polish on the remake of an Argentine film, a day or two's work sprucing up dialog for some piece of artsy Polish crap. You have anything on for next Thursday?"

"Thursday's good."

"Gustavo's? Around six? I'll bring a bottle of the good stuff."

That was Manny's one concession to success: he loved good wine. He'd show up with a bottle of Merlot from Chile, a blend of Merlot and Shiraz from Australia. Sit there in the wardrobe he'd paid out maybe ten dollars for at the nearest secondhand store six years ago and pour out this amazing stuff.

Even as he thought of it, Driver could taste Gustavo's slow-cooked pork and yucca. That made him hungry. Also made him remember the slug line of another, far classier L.A. restaurant: We season our garlic with food. At Gustavo's, the couple dozen chairs and half as many tables had set them back maybe a hundred dollars total, cases of meat and cheese sat in plain view, and it'd been a while since the walls got wiped down. But yeah, that pretty much said it. We season our garlic with food.

Driver went back to the counter, drank his cold coffee. Had another cup, hot, that wasn't much better.

At Benito's just down the block he ordered a burrito with machaca, piled on sliced tomatoes and jalapenos from the condiment bar. Something with taste. The jukebox belted out your basic Hispanic homeboy music, guitar and bajo sexto saying how it's always been, accordion fluttering open and closed like the heart's own chambers.

Chapter Three

Up till the time Driver got his growth about twelve, he was small for his age, an attribute of which his father made full use. The boy could fit easily through small openings, bathroom windows, pet doors and so on, making him a considerable helpmate at his father's trade, which happened to be burglary. When he did get his growth he got it all at once, shooting up from just below four feet to six-two almost overnight, it seemed. He'd been something of a stranger to and in his body ever since. When he walked, his arms flailed about and he shambled. If he tried to run, often as not he'd trip and fall over. One thing he could do, though, was drive. And he drove like a son of a bitch.

Once he'd got his growth, his father had little use for him. His father had had little use for his mother for a lot longer. So Driver wasn't surprised when one night at the dinner table she went after his old man with butcher and bread knives, one in each fist like a ninja in a red-checked apron. She had one ear off and a wide red mouth drawn in his throat before he could set his coffee cup down. Driver watched, then went on eating his sandwich: Spam and mint jelly on toast. That was about the extent of his mother's cooking.

He'd always marvelled at the force of this docile, silent woman's attack—as though her entire life had gathered toward that single, sudden bolt of action. She wasn't good for much else afterwards. Driver did what he could. But eventually the state came in and prised her from the crusted filth of an overstuffed chair complete with antimacassar. Driver they packed off to foster parents, a Mr. and Mrs. Smith in Tucson who right up till the day he left registered surprise whenever he came through the front door or emerged from the tiny attic room where he lived like a wren.

A few days shy of his sixteenth birthday, Driver came down the stairs from that attic room with all his possessions in a duffel bag and the spare key to the Ford Galaxie he'd fished out of a kitchen drawer. Mr. Smith was at work, Mrs. Smith off conducting classes at Vacation Bible School where, two years back, before he'd stopped attending, Driver had consistently won prizes for memorizing the most scripture. It was mid-summer, unbearably hot up in his room, not a lot better down here. Drops of sweat fell onto the note as he wrote.

*I'm sorry about the car, but I have to have wheels.
I haven't taken anything else. Thank you for taking
me in, for everything you've done. I mean that.*

Throwing the duffel bag over the seat, he backed out
of the garage, pulled up by the stop sign at the end of
the street, and made a hard left to California.

Chapter Four

They met at a low-rent bar between Sunset and Holly-wood east of Highland. Uniformed Catholic schoolgirls waited for buses across from lace, leather and lingerie stores and shoe shops full of spike heels size fifteen and up. Driver knew the guy right away when he stepped through the door. Pressed khakis, dark T-shirt, sport coat. *De rigueur* gold wristwatch. Copse of rings at finger and ear. Soft jazz spread from the house tapes, a piano trio, possibly a quartet, something rhythmically slippery, eel-like, you could never quite get a hold on it.

New Guy grabbed a Johnny Walker black, neat. Driver stayed with what he had. They went to a table near the back.

"Got your name from Revell Hicks."

Driver nodded. "Good man."

"Getting harder and harder all the time to step around the amateurs, know what I'm saying? Everybody thinks he's bad, everybody thinks he makes the best spaghetti sauce, everybody thinks he's a good driver."

"You worked with Revell, I have to figure you're a pro."

"Same here." New Guy threw back his scotch. "Fact is, what I hear is you're the best."

"I am."

"Other thing I've heard is, you can be hard to work with."

"Not if we understand one another."

"What's to understand? It's my job. So I'm pit boss. I run the team, call all the shots. Either you sign on to the team or you don't."

"Then I don't."

"Fair enough. Your call…"

"Another sparkling opportunity gone down the tubes."

"Let me buy you another drink, at least."

He went to the bar for a new round.

"I do have to wonder, though," he said, setting down a fresh beer and shot. "Care to enlighten me?"

"I drive. That's *all* I do. I don't sit in while you're planning the score or while you're running it down. You tell me where we start, where we're headed, where we'll be going afterwards, what time of day. I don't take part, I don't know anyone, I don't carry weapons. I drive."

"Attitude like that has to cut down something fierce on offers."

"It's not attitude, it's principle. I turn down a lot more work than I take."

"This one's sweet."

"They always are."

"Not like this."

Driver shrugged.

One of those rich communities north of Phoenix, New Guy said, a seven-hour drive, acre upon acre of half-a-mill homes like rabbit warrens, crowding out the desert's cactus. Writing something on a piece of paper, he pushed it across the table with two fingers. Driver remembered car salesmen doing that. People were so goddamned stupid. Who with any kind of pride, any sense of self, is gonna go along with that? What kind of fool would even put up with it?

"This is a joke, right?" Driver said.

"You don't want to participate, don't want a cut, there it is. Fee for service. We keep it simple."

Driver threw back his shot and pushed the beer across. Dance with the one who bought you. "Sorry to have wasted your time."

"Help if I add a zero to it?"

"Add three."

"No one's that good."

"Like you said, plenty of drivers out there. Take your pick."

"I think I just did." He nodded Driver back into the chair, pushed the beer towards him. "I'm just messing with you, man, checking you out." He fingered the small hoop in his right ear. Later, Driver decided that was probably a tell. "Four on the team, we split five ways. Two shares for me, one for each of the rest of you. That work?"

"I can live with it."

"So we have a deal."

"We do."

"Good. You up for another shot?"

"Why not?"

Just as the alto sax jumped on the tune's tailgate for a long, slow ride.

Chapter Five

Walking away from Benito's, Driver stepped into a world transformed. Like most cities, L.A. became a different beast by night. Final washes of pink and orange lay low on the horizon now, breaking up, fading, as the sun let go its hold and the city's lights, a hundred thousand impatient understudies, stepped in. Three guys with skinned heads and baseball caps flanked his car. Couldn't have looked like much to them. An unprepossessing 80's Ford. Without popping the hood they'd have no way of knowing what had been done to it. But here they were.

Driver walked to the door and stood waiting.

"Cool ride, man," one of the young toughs said, sliding off the hood. He looked at his buddies. They all laughed.

What a hoot.

Driver had the keys bunched in his hand, one braced and protruding between second and third fingers. Stepping directly forward, he punched his fist at alpha dog's windpipe, feeling the key tear through layers of flesh, looking down as he lay gasping for air.

In his rear view mirror he watched the young tough's buddies stand over him flapping hands and lips and trying to decide what the hell to do. It wasn't supposed to go down like this.

Maybe he should turn around. Go back and tell them that's what life was, a long series of things that didn't go down the way you thought they would.

Hell with it. Either they'd figure it out or they wouldn't. Most people never did.

Home was relative, of course, but that's where he went. Driver moved every few months. In that regard things hadn't changed much from the time he inhabited Mr. and Mrs. Smith's attic room. He existed a step or two to one side of the common world, largely out of sight, a shadow, all but invisible. Whatever he owned, either he could hoist it on his back and lug it along or he could walk away from it. Anonymity was the thing he loved most about the city, being a part of it and apart from it at the same time. He favored older apartment complexes where parking lots were cracked and stained with oil, where when the guy a few doors down played his music too loud you weren't about to complain, where frequently tenants loaded up in the middle of the night and rode off never to be heard from again. Even cops didn't like coming into such places.

His current apartment was on the second floor. From the front the dedicated stairway looked to be the only way up and down. But the back opened onto a general gallery, balconies running the length of each level, stairwells every third unit. A claustrophobic entryway just inside the door broke off to a living room on the right, bedroom to the left, kitchen tucked like a bird's head under wing behind the living room. With care you could store a coffeemaker and two or three cookpans in there, maybe half a run of dishes and a set of mugs, and still have room to turn around.

Which Driver did, putting a pan of water on to boil, coming back out to look across at blank windows directly opposite. Anyone live over there? Had an inhabited look somehow, but he'd yet to see any movement, any signs of life. A family of five lived in the apartment below. Seemed like whatever time of day or night he looked, two or more of them sat watching TV. A single man dwelled to the right, one of the studio apartments. He came home every night at five-forty with a six-pack and dinner in a white bag. Sat staring at the wall and pulling steadily at the beers, one every half-hour. Third beer, he'd finger out the burger and munch down. Then he'd drink the rest of the beers, and when they were gone he'd go to bed.

For a week or two when Driver first moved in, a woman of indeterminate age lived in the unit to the left. Mornings, post shower, she'd sit at the kitchen table rubbing lotion into her legs. Evenings, again nude or nearly so, she'd sit speaking for hours on a portable phone. Once Driver had watched as she threw the phone forcibly across the room. She stepped up to the window then, breasts flattening against the glass. Tears in her eyes—or had he just imagined that? He never saw her again after that night.

Returning to the kitchen, Driver poured boiling water over ground coffee in a filtered cone.

Someone was knocking at his door?

This absolutely did *not* happen. People who lived in places like Palm Shadows rarely mixed, and had good reason to expect no visitors.

"Smells good," she said when he went to the door. Thirtyish. Jeans looking as though small explosions had taken place here and there, outwards puffs of white showing. An oversize T-shirt, black, legend long since faded, only random letters, an F, an A, a few half con- sonants remaining. Six inches of blonde hair with a half-inch of dark backing it up.

"I just moved in down the hall."

A long narrow hand, curiously footlike, appeared before him. He took it.

"Trudy."

He didn't ask what white bread like her was doing here. He did wonder about the accent. Alabama, maybe?

"Heard your radio, that's how I knew you were home. Had myself a batch of cornbread all but ready to go when it came to me I didn't have a single egg, not a one. Any chance—"

"Sorry. There's a Korean grocer half a block up."

"Thanks....Think I could come in?"

Driver stepped aside.

"I like to know my neighbors."

"You're probably in the wrong place for that."

"Wouldn't be the first time. I have a history of bad choices. A downright talent for them."

"Can I get you something? I think there may be a beer or two left in the fridge—what you'd probably call the icebox."

"Why would I call it that?"

"I thought—"

"Some of that coffee I smelled would be great, actually."

Driver went into the kitchen, poured two mugs, brought them back.

"Kind of a strange place to live," she said.

"L.A.?"

"Here, I meant."

"I guess."

"Guy below me's always peeking out his door when I come in. Apartment next to me, their TV's going twenty-four hours a day. Spanish channel. Salsa, soap operas with half the characters getting killed and the rest screaming, godawful comedy shows with fat men in pink suits."

"See you're fitting right in."

She laughed. They sat quietly sipping coffee, chattering on about nothing in particular. Driver hadn't developed the capacity for small talk, could never see the point of it. Nor had he ever had much sensitivity to what others were feeling. But now he found himself talking openly about his parents and sensing, in his momentary companion, some deep pain that might never be lessened.

"Thanks for the coffee," she said at length. "For the conversation even more. But I'm fading fast."

"Stamina's the first thing to go."

They walked together to the door. That long, narrow hand came out again, and he took it.

"I'm in 2-G. I work nights, so I'm home all day. Maybe you'll come by sometime."

She waited and, when he said nothing, turned and walked away down the hall. Hips and rear end a marvel in her jeans. Growing ever smaller in the distance. Carrying that pain and sadness back with her to the lair where it, and she, lived.

Chapter Six

Second job he ever drove on, everything went wrong that could. Guys had passed themselves off as pros. They weren't.

The mark was a pawn shop out towards Santa Monica, near the airport, by a couple of buildings that put you in mind of old time computer punch cards. Shop wasn't much to look at if you went in the front door, the usual accordions, bikes, stereos, jewelry and junk. All the good stuff went in and out the back door. The money to pay the toll on that back door was stashed in a safe so old that Doc Holliday could have kept his dental tools in it.

They didn't need any accordions or jewelry. Money in that safe was another thing.

He was driving a Ford Galaxie. Right off the line this thing had more power than made any kind of sense, and he'd been seriously under the hood. From an alley alongside, he watched the principals, two of whom he figured as brothers, head towards the pawn shop. Minutes later, he heard the shots, like whip cracks. *One. Two. Three.* Then a sound like a cannon going off and a window blowing out somewhere. When he felt a load hit the car behind him, without even looking to see, he peeled out. Half a dozen blocks away, cops pulled in hard behind, two cars at first, then three, but they didn't have much chance against the Galaxie or the route he'd mapped out—not to mention his driving—and he soon lost them. When it was all over he discovered he'd got away with two of the three principals.

Fucker pulled a shotgun on us, you believe it? A fuckin' shotgun.

One of the presumed brothers they'd left behind, shot dead or dying on the pawn shop floor.

They'd also left the fuckin' money behind.

Chapter Seven

He wasn't supposed to have the money. He wasn't supposed to be a part of it at all. And he damned well ought to be back at work doing double-eights and turnarounds. Jimmie, his agent, probably had a stack of calls for him. Not to mention the shoot he was supposed to be working on. The sequences didn't make much sense to him, but they rarely did. He never saw scripts; like a session musician, he worked from chord charts. He suspected the sequences wouldn't make a lot more sense to the audience if they ever stopped to think about them. But they had flash aplenty. Meanwhile all he had to do was show up, hit the mark, do the trick—"deliver the goods," as Jimmie put it. Which he always did. In spades.

That Italian guy with all the forehead creases and warts was on the shoot, starring. Driver didn't go to movies much and could never quite remember his name, but he'd worked with him a couple of times before. Always brought his coffeemaker with him, slammed espressos the whole day like cough drops. Sometimes his mother showed up and got escorted around like she was queen.

That's what he was *supposed* to be doing.

But here he was.

The score'd been set for nine that morning, just after opening. Seemed ages ago now. Four in the crew. The cook—New Guy—who'd put it together, engineer and pit boss. Fresh muscle up from Houston by the name of Dave Strong. Been a Ranger, supposedly, in the Gulf War. The girl, Blanche. Him driving, of course. They'd pulled out of L.A. at midnight. All of it pretty straightforward: Blanche would set up the room, grab and hold attention, as Cook and Strong moved in.

Driver'd been out three days before to get a car. He always picked his own car. The cars weren't stolen, which was the first mistake people made, pros and amateurs alike. Instead, he bought them off small lots. You looked for something bland, something that would fade into the background. But you also wanted a ride that could get up on its rear wheels and paw air if you needed it to. Himself, he had a preference for older Buicks, mid-range, some shade of brown or gray, but he wasn't locked in. This time what he found was a ten-year-old Dodge. You could run this thing into the side of a tank with no effect. Drop anvils on it, they'd bounce off. But when he turned the motor over, it was like this honey was just clearing its throat, getting ready to talk.

"Got a back seat for it?" he asked the salesman who'd gone along on the test drive. You didn't have to push the car, just turn it loose, see where it went. Watch and feel how it cornered, if its center stayed put when you accelerated, slowed, cut in or out. Most of all, listen. First thing he'd done was turn off the radio. Then, a couple of times, he had to hush the salesman. There was a little too much play in the transmission for his taste. Clutch needed to come up some. And it pulled to the right. But otherwise it was about as perfect as he had any right to expect. Back at the lot, he crawled underneath to be sure the carriage was straight, axles and ties in good shape. Then asked about the back seat.

"We can find you one."

He paid the man cash and drove it off the lot to one of several garages he used. They'd give it the works, new tires, oil and lube, new belts and hoses, a tune-up, then store it, where it would be out of sight till he picked it up for the job.

Next day, his call was at six a.m., which in Hollywoodese translated to show up around eight. Guy working second unit held out for a quick take (why wouldn't he, that's what he got paid for) but Driver insisted on a trial run. Buggy they gave him was a white-over-aqua '58 Chevy. Looked cherry, but it drove like a goddamned mango. First run, he missed the last mark by half a yard.

Good enough, the second-unit guy said.

Not for me, Driver told him.

Man, Second Unit came back, this is what? ninety seconds in a film that lasts two hours? That rocked!

Plenty of other drivers out there, Driver told him. Make the call.

Second run went like a song. Driver gave himself a little more time to get up to speed, hit the ramp to go up on two wheels as he sailed through the alley, came back down onto four and into a moonshiner's turn to face the way he'd come. The ramp would be erased in editing, and the alley would look a lot longer than it was.

The crew applauded.

He had one other scene blocked for the day, a simple run against traffic down an interstate. By the time the crew finished setting up, always the most complicated part, it was coming onto two in the afternoon. Driver nailed it on the first run. Two-twenty-three, and the rest of the day belonged to him.

He caught a double-header of Mexican movies out on Pico, downed a couple of slow beers at a bar nearby making polite conversation with the guy on the next stool, then had dinner at the Salvadoran restaurant up the street from his current crib, rice cooked with shrimp and chicken, fat tortillas with that great bean dip they do, sliced cucumbers, radish and tomatoes.

By then he'd killed most of the evening, which is pretty much what he aimed for when he wasn't working one job or the other. But even after a bath and half a glass of scotch he couldn't get to sleep.

Now he knew: that was something he should have paid attention to.

Life sends us messages all the time—then sits around laughing over how we're not gonna be able to figure them out.

So at three a.m. he's looking out the window at the loading dock across the street thinking no way the crew over there, hauling stuff out of the warehouse and tucking it away in various trucks, is legit. There's no activity anywhere else on the dock, no job boss or lights, and they're moving at a good, nonunion pace.

He thinks about calling the police, see how that plays out, watch while it all got a lot more interesting. But he doesn't.

Around five, he pulled on jeans and an old sweatshirt and went out for breakfast at the Greek's.

◇◇◇

Things go wrong on a job, sometimes it starts so subtly you don't see it at first. Other times, it's all dominoes and fireworks.

This was somewhere in between.

Sitting in the Dodge pretending to read a newspaper, Driver watched the others enter. There'd been a small line waiting outside the door, five or six people. He could see them all through the blinds. Blanche chatting with the security guard just inside the door, brushing hair back from her face. Other two looking around, at the point of putting guns in the mix. Everyone still smiling, for now.

Driver also watched:

An old man sitting on the low brick wall across from the storefront, knees stuck up like a grasshopper's, struggling to get his breath;

Two kids, twelve or so, skateboarding down the sidewalk opposite;

The usual pack of suit-and-dress people heading for work clutching briefcases and shoulder bags, looking tired already;

An attractive, well-dressed woman perhaps forty years old walking a boxer from both sides of whose mouth strings of gluey saliva hung;

A muscular Latino offloading crates of vegetables from his double-parked pickup to a Middle Eastern restaurant down the block;

A Chevy in the narrow alley three storefronts down.

That one brought him up short. It was like looking in a mirror. Car sitting there, driver inside, eyes moving right to left, up, down. Didn't fit the scene at all. Absolutely no reason for that car to be where it was.

Then sudden motion inside caught his attention— everything happened fast, he'd put the pieces together later—and Driver saw the backup guy, Strong, turn toward Blanche, lips moving. Watched him go down as she drew and fired before hitting the floor as though she'd been shot herself. Cook, the guy who'd put it all together, had begun firing in her direction.

He was still thinking *What the fuck?* when Blanche came barreling out with the bag of money and threw it onto the new back seat.

Drive!

Drive he did, pulling out in a brake-accelerator skid between a FedEx truck and a Volvo with a couple dozen dolls on the shelf by the rear windshield and a license plate that read *Urthship2*, not at all surprised to find the Chevy wheeling in behind him as he watched Urthship2 crash-land into the sidewalk bins of a secondhand book-and-records store.

Air would be thin up there for Urthship2, the new world's natives hostile.

The Chevy stayed with them for a long time—the guy was that good—as Blanche sat beside him hauling money by the handful out of the gym bag, shaking her head and going *Shit! Oh shit!*

The suburbs saved them, just as they saved so many others from the city's damning influence. Finding his way to the subdivision he'd scouted earlier, Driver barreled onto a quiet residential street, tapping the brakes once, again, then again, so that by the time he reached the speed trap he was cruising a steady, sure twenty-five.

Not knowing the area and not wanting to lose them, the Chevy had come charging in. Driver watched in the rear view mirror as local cops pulled it over. Squad pulled up at an angle behind, motorcycle mountie in front. Guys would be telling this story back at the station for weeks.

Shit, Blanche said beside him. *There's a lot more money here than there oughta be. Has to be close to a quarter of a million. Oh shit!*

Chapter Eight

As a kid, new to town, he'd hung around the studio lots. So did a bunch of others, all ages, all types. But it wasn't the stars in their limos or supporting players arriving in Mercedes and BMWs he was interested in, it was the guys who sailed in on Harleys, muscle cars and jacked-up pickups. As always he stayed quiet, hung back, kept his ear to the ground. A shadow. Before long he'd heard word of a bar and grill these guys favored in the grungiest part of old Hollywood, and started hanging out there instead. Some time in the second week, two or three in the afternoon, he looked up to see Shannon settling in at one end of the bar. The barkeep greeted him by name and had a beer and shot in front of him damned near before he sat down.

Shannon had a first name no one used. It got listed on credits, nether end of the scroll; that was about it. Up from somewhere in the South, hill country, everyone said. The Scots-Irish ancestry of so many of those hill folk showed in Shannon's features, complexion and voice. But what he most looked like was your typical redneck from Alabama.

He was the best stunt driver in the business.

"Keep 'em coming," Shannon told the barkeep.

"You need to tell me that?"

He'd sucked three mugs dry and thrown back as many shots of well bourbon by the time Driver worked up courage enough to approach him. Stopped with the fourth shot glass on the way to his mouth as Driver stood there.

"Help you with something, kid?"

A kid not much older (he was thinking) than those streaming home from school now in buses, cars and limos.

"Thought maybe I could buy you a drink or two."

"You did, did you?" He went ahead and tossed the shot back, set the glass gently on the bar. "Soles of your shoes are mostly gone. Clothes don't look much better, and I'd wager that backpack holds damn near everything you own. Been some time since you and water touched base. Plus you probably haven't eaten in a day or two. Am I on track here?"

"Yes sir."

"But you want to buy me a drink."

"Yes sir."

"You'll do just fine here in L.A.," Shannon said, gulping a third of his beer. Signaled the barkeep, who was there instantly.

"Give this young man whatever he wants to drink, Eddie. And have the kitchen send out a burger, double fries, coleslaw."

"Got it." Scribbling on an order pad, Danny tore off the top sheet and clipped it with a wooden clothes pin to a hoop he then spun towards the kitchen. A hand back there reached for it. Driver said a beer would be fine.

"What do you want from me, boy?"

"My name's—"

"Hard as it may be for you to believe this, I don't give a flying fuck what your name is."

"I'm from—"

"And I care even less about that."

"Tough audience."

"Audiences are. That's their nature."

Danny was there with food not long after, never a long turnaround, places like this. He set the platter down before Shannon, who inclined his head towards Driver.

"For the kid. I, on the other hand, could use another couple soldiers."

The plate slid his way and Driver tucked in, thanking them both. The bun was soggy with grease from the burger, fries crisp on the outside and meaty beneath, coleslaw creamy and sweet. Shannon nursed his beer this time. While the shot stood patiently by, waiting.

"How long have you been out here, boy?"

"Better part of a month, I guess. Hard to keep track."

"This the first square meal you've had in that time?"

"I had some money, to start with. It didn't last long."

"Never does. In this city more than most." He allowed himself a measured sip of bourbon. "Tomorrow, the next day, you're going to be every bit as hungry as you were ten minutes ago. What are you gonna do then? Roll tourists on Sunset for the few dollars they have on them and traveler's checks you won't be able to cash? Hit convenience stores, maybe? We've got career professionals for that."

"I'm good with cars."

"Well then, there you go. Good mechanic can get a job anywhere, anytime."

Not that he couldn't do that, Driver told him. He was damned near as good under the hood as he was behind the wheel. But what he did best, what he did better than just about anyone else was, he drove.

Finishing off his shot, Shannon laughed.

"Been a long time since I took to remembering how that felt," he said. "Feeling so full of yourself, so confident. Thinking you can eat the world. You really that sure of yourself, kid?"

Driver nodded.

"Good. You want any kind of life out here, you even expect to survive, not get eaten up, used up, you damn well better be."

Shannon finished his beer, settled the tab, and asked if Driver'd care to come along. Dipping into the six-pack Shannon had bought off Eddie, they drove for a half-hour or so before Shannon nosed the Camaro over a low ridge and down a slope into a system of drainage canals.

Driver looked about. A landscape not all that different, really, from the Sonoran desert where, in Mr. Smith's ancient Ford truck, he'd taught himself to drive. Bare flatland ringed by culvert walls, an array of shopping carts, garbage bags, tires and small appliances not unlike the random saguaro, scrub and cholla he'd learned to maneuver about.

Shannon pulled up and stepped out of the car, left the motor running. Last couple of beers dangled in their plastic web from his hand.

"Here's your chance, kid. Show me what you have."

So he did.

Afterwards they went for Mexican food to a place on Sepulveda the size of a train boxcar where everyone, waitress, busboy, cook, seemed to be family. They all knew him, and Shannon spoke to them in what Driver later discovered was perfect idiomatic Spanish. He and Shannon had a couple of scotches to start, chips and salsa, a blistering caldo, green enchiladas. By the end of the meal, several Pacificos having passed by on parade, Driver was fairly wiped.

That morning he woke up on Shannon's couch, where he lived for the next four months. Two days later he had his first job, a fairly standard chase scene in a low-end cop show. Script had him hitting a corner, taking it on two wheels, coming back down—simple, straightforward stuff. But just as he pulled into the turn Driver saw what could be done here. Swinging in closer to the wall, he dropped those airborne wheels onto the wall. Looked like he'd left the ground and was driving horizontally.

"Holy shit!" the second-unit director was heard to say. "For God's sake print that—now!"

A reputation was being born.

Standing in the shadow of one of the trailers, Shannon smiled. *That's my boy.* He was working a top-grade movie four stages over, swung by on a break to see how the kid was doing.

The kid was doing all right. The kid was still doing all right ten months later when, on a perfectly routine call, a stunt the like of which he'd done a hundred times, Shannon's car went over the edge of the canyon he was speeding along and, cameras rolling, catching the whole thing, plunged a hundred yards straight down, somersaulted twice, and sat rocking on its back like a beetle.

Chapter Nine

"I'm gonna run across and grab something to eat," Blanche said. "I saw a Pizza Hut over there and I'm starved. Sausage and extra cheese okay?"

"Sure," he said, standing near the door, by one of those picture windows on aluminum tracks that all motels seem to have. The lower left corner had sprung out of the frame and he could feel warm air from outside pouring in. They were in a second-floor room facing front, with only the balcony, stairway and twenty yards or so of parking lot between them and the interstate. The motel itself had three separate exits. One ramp onto the interstate was off the intersection beyond the parking lot. Another was just up the street.

First thing you do, room, bar, restaurant, town or crib, is check and memorize the ways out.

Earlier, road weary, bodies vibrating from far too many hours in the car, they'd watched a movie on TV, a caper film set in Mexico with an actor who'd been big for about three days before sinking into drugs, guest-star gigs in films like this one shot on the cheap, and the meager, trailing fame of tabloid headlines.

Driver marveled at the power of our collective dreams. Everything gone to hell, the two of them become running dogs, and what do they do? They sit there watching a movie. Couple of chase scenes, Driver'd be willing to swear it was Shannon driving. Never saw him, of course. But definitely his style.

Has to be Blanche, Driver thought, standing by the window. *No other way that Chevy was down there in the parking lot.*

She'd taken a brush out of her purse and started into the bathroom.

He heard her say "What—"

Then the dull boom of the shotgun.

Driver went in around Blanche's body, saw the man in the window, then slipped in blood and slammed into the shower stall, shattering the glass door and ripping his arm open. The man still struggled to free himself. But now he was lifting the gun again and swinging it towards Driver, who, without thinking, picked up a piece of the jagged glass and threw. It hit the man full on in the forehead. Pink flesh flowered there, blood poured into the man's eyes, and he dropped the shotgun. Driver saw the razor by the sink. He used it.

The other one was doing his best to kick the door in. That's what Driver had been hearing all along without realizing what it was, that dull drumming sound. He broke through just as Driver came back into the room—just in time for the shotgun's second load. Thing was maybe twenty inches long and it kicked like a son of a bitch, doing more damage to his arm. Driver could see flesh and muscle and bone in there.

Not that he was complaining, mind you.

◇◇◇

Sitting with his back against the wall in a Motel 6 just north of Phoenix, Driver watched blood lapping toward him. Traffic sounds rolled in from the interstate. Someone wept in the next room. He realized he'd been holding his breath, listening for sirens, for the sound of people gathering on stairways or down in the parking lot, for the scramble of feet beyond the door, and took a deep draw of room air gone foul with the smell of blood, urine, feces, cordite, fear.

Neon flashed on the skin of the tall, pale man near the door.

He heard the drip of the tub's faucet from the bathroom.

He heard something else as well, a scratching, a scrabbling, more drumlike sounds. Realized at length that it was his own arm jumping involuntarily, knuckles rapping at the floor, fingers scratching and thumping as the hand contracted.

The arm hung there, apart from him, unconnected, like an abandoned shoe. When Driver willed it to move, nothing happened.

Worry about that later.

He looked back at the open door. Maybe that's it, Driver thought. Maybe no one else is coming, maybe it's over. Maybe, for now, three bodies are enough.

Chapter Ten

After four months at Shannon's he'd put away enough money to move out to his own place, an apartment complex in old east Hollywood. The check Driver wrote for deposit and rent was the first he'd written in his life and among the last. Soon enough he learned to operate on cash, stay off the radar, leave as few footprints as possible. "Good God, we're in a Forties movie," Shannon said when he saw the place. "Which apartment's Marlowe live in?" Except that, these days, sitting out on the plank-like balcony, one heard far more Spanish than English.

He'd been coming up the stairs when the door next to his opened and a woman asked, in perfect English but with the unmistakable lilt of a native Spanish speaker, if he needed any help.

Seeing her, a Latina roughly his age, hair like a raven's wing, eyes alight, he wished to hell he did need help. But what he had in his arms was about everything he owned.

"How about a beer, then?" she asked when he admitted to it. "Help you recover from all that heavy lifting."

"That, I could do."

"Good. I'm Irina. Come over whenever you're ready. I'll leave the door ajar."

Minutes later, he stepped into her apartment, a mirror image, really, of his own. Soft music playing in three-quarter time, something with accordion fills and frequent appearances of the word *corazon*. Driver remembered once hearing a jazz musician claim that waltz time was the closest thing to the rhythm of the human heart. Sitting on a couch identical to his though considerably cleaner and more worn, Irina watched a soap opera on one of the Spanish-language TV channels. Novellas, they called them. They were huge.

"Beer on the table here, you want it."

"Thanks."

Settling onto the couch beside her, he smelled her perfume, smelled the morning's soap and shampoo and the smell of her body beneath, subtler and solider at the same time.

"New in town?" she asked.

"Been here a few months. Staying with a friend till now."

"Where are you from?"

"Tucson."

Expecting the usual remarks about cowboys, he was surprised when she said, "I've got a couple of uncles and their families living out there. South Tucson, I think they call it? Haven't seen them in years."

"That's a world apart, South Tucson."

"Like L.A. isn't?"

It was for him.

How much more for her?

Or for this child that came staggering sleepily out of the bedroom.

"Yours?" he said.

"These tend to come with the apartment. Place is overrun with roaches and children. Probably want to check your closets, look under kitchen counters."

She stood, scooped the child up on one arm.

"This is Benicio."

"I'm four," the boy said.

"And very stubborn about going to bed."

"How old are *you*?" Benicio asked.

"Good question. Okay if I call *my* mom, check in with her about this?"

"Meanwhile," Irina said, "we'll get you a cookie and a glass of milk out in the kitchen."

Minutes later, they returned.

"Well?" Benicio said.

"Twenty, I'm afraid," Driver told him. He wasn't, but that's what he was telling the world.

"Old." Just as he'd suspected.

"Sorry. Maybe we can still be friends, though?"

"Maybe."

"Your mother's alive?" Irina asked once she'd tucked the boy back in.

Easier to say no than to explain it all.

She told him she was sorry, and moments later asked what he did for a living.

"You first."

"Here in the promised land? A three-star career. Mondays through Fridays I waitress at a Salvadoran restaurant on Broadway for minimum wage plus tips—tips from people little better off than myself. Three nights a week I do maid service for homes and apartments in Brentwood. Weekends I sweep and vacuum office buildings. Your turn."

"I'm in the movies."

"Sure you are."

"I'm a driver."

"Like for limos, right?"

"A stunt driver."

"You mean all those car chases and stuff?"

"That's me."

"Wow. You must get paid good for that."

"Not really. But it's steady work."

Driver told her how Shannon had taken him under wing, taught him what he needed to know, got him his first jobs.

"You're lucky to have someone like that in your life. I never did."

"What about Benicio's father?"

"We were married for about ten minutes. His name is Standard Guzman. First time I met him I asked, 'Well, is there a deluxe Guzman somewhere around?' and he just looked at me, didn't get it at all."

"What's he do?"

"Lately he's been into charity work, helping provide jobs for state workers."

Driver was lost. Seeing his expression, she added: "He's inside."

"Prison, you mean?"

"That's what I mean."

"How long?"

"Be out next month."

On TV, beneath the looming, half-exposed breasts of his blonde assistant, a stubby dark guy in a silver lamé frock coat performed parlor magic. Balls between upturned cups appeared and vanished, cards leapt from the deck, doves flapped up from chafing pans.

"He's a thief—a professional, he keeps telling me. Started off burglarizing homes when he was fourteen, fifteen, moved on from there. They got him taking down a savings and loan. Couple of local detectives happened to walk into the middle of it. They'd come to deposit their paychecks."

Standard did indeed get out the following month. And despite all Irina's protests that this would *not* happen, no way in godalmighty hell, he came home to roost. (What can I say? she said. He loves the boy. Where else is he gonna go?) She and Driver were hanging together a lot by then, which didn't bother Standard at all. Most nights, long after Irina and Benicio had gone to bed, Driver and Standard would sit out in the front room watching TV. Lot of the good, old stuff you only caught then, late at night.

So once, along about one on a Tuesday night, Wednesday morning really, they're sitting there watching a cop movie, *Glass Ceiling*, and a commercial comes on.

"Rina tells me you drive. For the movies?"

"Right."

"Have to be pretty good."

"I get by."

"Not like a nine-to-five gig, huh?"

"One of the advantages."

"You have anything on for tomorrow? *Today* now, I guess it is?"

"Nothing scheduled."

Having found its way past a thicket of commercials for furniture dealers, bedding stores, cut-rate insurance, twenty-piece cooking sets and videocassettes of great moments in American history, the movie started up again.

"I'm thinking I can speak frankly with you," Standard said.

Driver nodded.

"Rina trusts you, I figure I can too….You want another beer?"

"Usually."

He went out to the kitchen and brought two back. Snapped the tab off one and handed it over.

"You know what I do, right?"

"More or less."

Snapped the tab and took a swallow of his.

"Okay. So here's the thing. I've got a job today, something that's been on the burner a long time. But my driver's been…well, detained."

"Like this guy," Driver said, nodding towards the TV, where a suspect was being interrogated. The front legs of the chair on which he sat had been cut down to make it as uncomfortable as possible.

"Good chance of it. What I'm wondering is, any chance you'd consider taking his place?"

"Driving?"

"Right. We go in early morning. It's—"

Driver held up a hand.

"I don't need to know, don't want to know. I'll drive for you. That's all I'll do."

"Fair enough."

Three or four more minutes of movie action, and commercials shouldered back in. Miracle stove-top grill. Commemorative plates. Greatest hits.

"I ever tell you how much Rina and Benicio depend on you?"

"I ever tell you what an asshole you are?"

"Nah," Standard said. "But that's okay, just about everybody else has."

They both laughed.

Chapter Eleven

That first run, Driver netted close to three thousand.

"Anything up?" he asked Jimmie, his agent, the next day.

"Couple of calls about to go out."

"Cattle calls, you're saying."

"Okay."

"And for this I pay you fifteen percent?"

"Welcome to the promised land."

"Locusts and all."

But by day's end he had two jobs lined up. Word was getting around, Jimmie told him. Not just that he could drive, the town was full of people who could drive, but word that he'd be there when they needed him, never watched the clock, never made waves, always delivered. They know you're a pro, not some hardass or punk out to make a name for himself, Jimmie said, you're who they're gonna ask for.

First shoot didn't pick up till next week, so Driver decided to head up Tucson way for a visit. He hadn't seen his mom since they pried her out of the chair long years past. He'd been little more than a kid then.

Why now? Hell if he knew.

As he drove, in a series of shudders the landscape changed about him. First the haphazard, old-town streets of central L.A. slowly giving way to the city's ever-incomprehensible network of ancillary cities and suburbs, then nothing much but interstate for a long time. Gas stations, Denny's, Del Tacos, discount malls, lumber yards. Trees, walls and fences. By this time the Galaxie had been traded in on a vintage Chevy with a hood you could land aircraft on and a backseat big enough for a small family to live in.

He stopped for breakfast at a Union 76 and watched the truckers sitting in their special section over plates of steak and eggs, roast beef, meatloaf, fried chicken, chicken-fried steak. Great American road food. Truckers, the final embodiment of America's enduring dream of absolute freedom, forever lighting out for the territory.

The building into whose parking lot he nosed the Chevy looked and smelled like the auxiliary buildings in which Sunday-School sessions had been held when he was a kid. Cheapest possible construction, dull white walls, unadorned cement floors.

"You're here to see...?"

"Sandra Daley."

The receptionist peered deeply into her screen. Fingers danced nimbly on a worn keyboard.

"I can't seem to—oh, here she is. You are...?"

"Her son."

She picked up her phone.

"Could you have a seat over there, sir? Someone will be with you shortly."

Within minutes a young Eurasian woman wearing a starched white lab coat, jeans beneath, came through locked doors. Low wooden heels ticked on the concrete floors.

"You're here to see Mrs. Daley?"

Driver nodded.

"And you're her son?"

He nodded again.

"I'm sorry. Do please forgive our caution. But records show that, all these years, Mrs. Daley has never had a visitor. Could I ask to see some ID?"

Driver displayed his driver's license. Those days he still had one that wasn't a double or triple blind.

Almond eyes scanned it.

"Again," she said, "I apologize."

"Not a problem."

Above almond eyes her eyebrows were natural, straight across with almost no arch, a bit unkempt. He always wondered why Latinas plucked theirs only to draw in thin arched substitutes. Change yourself, you change the world?

"I regret having to tell you this: your mother died last week. There were a number of other problems, but congestive heart failure is what finally took her. An alert nurse picked up the clinical change; within the hour we had her on a ventilator. But by then it was too late. It so often is."

She touched his shoulder.

"I'm sorry. We did our best to get in touch. Apparently what contact numbers we had were long since invalid." Her eyes swept his face, looking for cues. "Nothing I can say will be of much help, I'm afraid."

"It's okay, Doctor."

Brought up on tonal languages, she caught the slight rise in pitch at sentence's end. He hadn't even known it was there.

"Park," she said. "Doctor Park. Amy."

They both turned to watch as a gurney came into view down the corridor. Barge on the river. *African Queen.* A nurse sat astride the patient, pumping at his chest. "Shit!" she said. "Just felt a rib crack."

"I barely knew her. I just thought...."

"I really must go."

In the parking lot he leaned against the Chevy, stood looking off towards the mountain ranges ringing Tucson. Catalinas to the north, Santa Rita to the south, Rincon east, Tucson west. The whole city was a compass. How could anyone ever have gotten so hopelessly lost here?

Chapter Twelve

Second and third runs with Irina's husband went well. Driver's gym bag on the closet floor under shoes and dirty clothes fattened.

Then the next run.

Everything started out fine. Ducks in a row, all on track, according to plan. Target was a low-end, homegrown shop offering check cashing and payroll advances. It hunkered down at one spare end of a Sixties strip mall, next to an abandoned theater with posters for dubbed science fiction movies and foreign-made crime thrillers featuring out-of-work American actors still under glass. To the other side sat a pawn shop so erratically open it didn't even bother to post business hours. Its real business took place through the back door. Garlic, cumin, coriander and lemon from a falafel shop aromatized the region.

They'd gone in at nine, first opening. Metal shutters got pushed up then, doors unlocked. Only hired help about, workers getting minimum wage with no incentive to hold out or really give much of a shit, boss never around till ten or after. That time of day, even if there was an alarm, you could count on police being tapped out by rush-hour traffic.

Unfortunately, cops had the pawn shop staked out and one of them, terminally bored, happened to be looking at Check-R-Cash when Standard's crew went in. He had a thing for the tall Latina who manned the front desk.

"Well, shit."

"Wha's wrong, she don' love you no more?"

He told them. "So what do we do?" Not even close to what they'd been waiting for.

DeNoux being senior officer, it was his decision. He ran a hand through bristle-cut gray hair. "You guys as tired of this detail as I am?" he asked.

Tired of eating crap? Getting broiled all day in the van? Peeing in bottles? What's to be tired of?

"I hear you. What the fuck. Let's hit it."

Driver watched as the commandos burst out the van's back doors and charged Check-R-Cash. Knowing their attention was directed forward, he eased out from behind the Dumpster. Took him but moments out of the car, motor running, to slash the van's tires. Then he pulled up at the front of the store. Gunfire inside. Three had gone in. Two emerged to slam into the back seat as he popped the clutch, floored it, and shot out across the parking lot. One of the two who'd come out was mortally wounded.

Neither of them was Standard.

Chapter Thirteen

"You've had the pork and yucca, right?"

"Only about twenty times. Nice vest! New?"

"Everyone's a comic."

Even this early, a little before six, Gustavo's was packed. Manny squinted as Anselmo slipped a Modelo before him. Any time he left his cave the light was too strong.

"Gracias."

"How's the writing gig?"

"Hey, we're the same. Sit on our butts all day guiding things towards disaster. Car or script goes over the edge, we start again." He threw back his beer in a couple of gulps. "Enough of that shit. Let's have something good." Pulling a bottle out of his backpack. "New, from Argentina. Malbec grapes."

Anselmo materialized with wineglasses. Manny poured, slid a glass across. They both sipped.

"Am I right?" He had another taste. "Oh, yeah. I'm right." Holding onto the glass as onto a buoy, Manny looked about. "You ever think this was what your life would come to? Not that I know fuckall about your life."

"Not sure I ever thought much about it."

Manny held up his wineglass, peering across the liquid's dark surface, tilting the glass as though to bring the world to level.

"I was going to be the next great American writer. No doubt in my mind whatever. Had a shitload of stories in literary magazines. Then my first novel came out and gave credence to the Flat Earth folk—fell right off the edge of the world. Second one didn't even have energy enough left to scream as it went over. What about you?"

"Mostly I was just trying to get from Monday to Wednesday. Get out of my attic room, get out from under, get out of town."

"That's a lot of getting."

"That's ordinary life."

"I hate ordinary life."

"You hate everything."

"I take exception, sir. A gross misrepresentation. While it may be true that I possess a distaste for such offal as the American political system, Hollywood movies, New York publishing, our last half-dozen Presidents, every movie made in the last ten years excepting those of the Coen Brothers, newspapers, talk radio, American cars, the music industry, media hype, the latest hot thing—"

"Quite a catalog."

"—for many things in life I've an appreciation approaching reverence. This bottle of wine, for instance. The weather in L.A. Or the food to follow." He refilled their glasses. "You still getting steady work?"

"Mostly."

"Good. Not a total loss, then, moviemaking. Unlike many of today's parents, at least it provides for its own."

"Some of them."

True to form, the food was everything remembered and anticipated. They followed up at a nearby bar, beer for Driver, brandy for Manny. An old man who spoke little English wandered in with his battered accordion and sat playing tangos and the songs of his youth, songs of romance and of war, as patrons stood him drinks and dropped bills into his instrument case and tears ran down his cheeks.

By nine Manny's speech was slurring.

"So much for my big night out on the town. Used to be able to do this all night long."

"I can drive you home."

"Of course you can."

"Let me just put this out there," Manny said as they pulled up on the street outside his bungalow. "I have to be in New York next week. And I don't fly."

"Fly? You barely crawl."

So maybe Driver was feeling the drinks too.

"Be that as it may," Manny went on, "I was wondering if you'd consider driving me. I'd pay top dollar."

"Don't see how I can. I've got shoots scheduled. But even if I could, no way I'd ever take your money."

Having wrestled his way out of the car, Manny leaned back down to the window: "Just keep it in mind, okay?"

"Sure I will. Why not? Get some sleep, my friend."

Ten blocks away, a police unit hove up in his rear view mirror. Careful to maintain speed and to signal turns well in advance, Driver pulled into a Denny's and parked facing the street.

The cop went by. He was patrolling solo. Window rolled down, takeout cup of coffee from 7-Eleven in one hand, radio crackling.

Coffee sounded good.

Might as well have some while he was here.

Chapter Fourteen

From inside he heard the bleating of a terminally wounded saxophone. Doc had ideas about music different from most people's.

"Been a while," Driver said when the door opened to a nose like a bloated mushroom, soft-poached eyes.

"Seems like just yesterday," Doc said. "Course, to me *everything* seems like just yesterday. When I remember it at all."

Then he just stood there. The sax went on bleating behind him. He glanced back that way, and for a moment Driver thought he might be getting ready to yell over his shoulder for it to shut up.

"No one plays like that anymore," Doc said with a sigh.

He looked down.

"You're dripping on my welcome mat."

"You don't have a welcome mat."

"No—but I used to. A nice one. Then people somehow started getting the notion I meant it." That strangled sound—a laugh? "You could be the blood man, you know. Like the milk man. Making deliveries. People'd put out bottles with a list of what they need rolled up in the mouth. Half a pint of serum, two pints of whole, small container of packed cells....I don't need any blood, blood man."

"But *I* will, and a lot more besides, if you don't let me in."

Doc backed off, gap in the door widening. Man had been living in a garage when he and Driver first met. Here he was, still living in a garage. Bigger one, though; Driver'd give him that. Doc had spent half a lifetime dispensing marginally legal drugs to the Hollywood crowd before he got shut down and moved to Arizona. Had a mansion up in the Hills, people said, so many rooms that no one, even Doc himself, ever knew who was living there. Guests wandered up stairwells during parties and didn't show up again for days.

"Have a taste?" Doc asked, pouring from a half-gallon jug of generic bourbon.

"Why not?"

Doc handed him a half-filled water tumbler so bleary it might have been smeared with Vaseline.

"Cheers," Driver said.

"That arm doesn't look so good."

"You think?"

"You want, I could have a look at it."

"I didn't call ahead."

"I'll work you in."

Driver watched as dissembling fell away.

"Be good to be of use again."

Doc scurried about gathering things. Some of the things he gathered and laid out in a perfect line were a little scary.

Easing Driver out of his coat, scissoring blood-soaked shirt and pasty T-shirt away, Doc whistled tunelessly, squinting.

"Eyesight's not what it used to be." As he reached to probe at the wound with a hemostat, his hand shook. "But then again, what is?"

He smiled.

"Takes me right back. All those muscle groups. Used to read *Gray's Anatomy* obsessively when I was in high school. Lugged the damn thing around like a Bible."

"Following in your father's footsteps?"

"Not hardly. My old man was eighty-six per cent white bread and a hundred per cent asshole. Spent his life selling roomfuls of furniture on credit to families he knew couldn't afford it only so he could repossess it and go on charging them."

Pulling the top off a bottle of Betadine, Doc dumped it into a saucepan, found a packet of cotton squares and threw them in as well. Fished one out with two fingers.

"Mother was Peruvian. How the hell they ever met's beyond me, circles he traveled in. Back home she'd been a midwife and curandera. A healer. Important person in the community. Here, she got turned into goddam Donna Reed."

"By him?"

"Him. Society. America. Her own expectations. Who can say?"

Doc swabbed gently at the wound.

His hands had quit shaking.

"Medicine was the great love of my life, the only woman I ever needed or went after....Been a while, though—like you say. Sure hope I remember the how of it."

Yellowing teeth broke into a grin.

"Relax," he said. He swiveled a cheap desk lamp closer. "Just having my fun with you."

The bulb in the desk lamp flickered, failed, came back when Doc thumped it.

Taking a healthy swig himself, he handed Driver the jug of bourbon.

"Think that record's got a skip in it?" Doc said. "Sounds to me like it's been going round and round for some time."

Driver listened. How could you tell? Same phrase over and over. Kind of.

Doc nodded to the jug.

"Take a few more hits off that, boy. Chances are you'll need them. Probably both of us will, before this is over. You ready?"

No.

"Yes."

Chapter Fifteen

As always, the set-up took most of the time. Spend five hours on the prep, then you drive it in a minute and a half flat. Driver got paid the same for that five hours as he did for the minute and a half. If it was a high-end shoot, he'd been in the day before to check out the car and test-drive it. Budget variety, he'd do that first thing the day of the shoot, while the rest of the staff scrambled about like ants, getting in line. Then he'd spend his time hanging out with writers, script people and bit players, taking advantage of the buffet table. Even on a "wee small" film (as Shannon described them) there'd be enough food to feed a midsize town. Cold cuts, various cheeses, fruit, pizza, canapés, bite-size hot dogs in barbecue sauce, doughnuts and sweet rolls and Danish, sandwiches, boiled eggs, chips, salsa, onion dip, granola, juices and bottled water, coffee, tea, milk, energy drinks, cookies, cakes.

Today he was driving an Impala and the sequence was: double-vehicle ram, bootlegger's turn, moonshiner's turn, sideswipe. Ordinarily they'd break it down to segments, but the director wanted to try for a straight shoot in real time.

Driver was on the run. Coming over a hill he'd see a blockade, two State Police cars pulled in nose to nose.

What you do is start off from almost a full stop, car in low gear. You come in from the right, a quarter of a car-width or so—just like finding the pocket by the headpin for a strike. Gas to the floor, you're going between fifteen and thirty mph when you hit.

And it worked like a charm. The two State Police cars sprang apart, the Impala shot through with a satisfying fishtail and squeal of tires as Driver regained traction and floored it.

But it wasn't over. A third cop car lugged down the hill. Seeing what happened, he'd jumped the road up there and now came sliding and crashing down through trees, throwing up divots of soil and vegetation, bottoming out more than once, hitting the road fifty yards behind.

Driver let off the gas, dropping to twenty-five, maybe thirty mph, then hauled the steering wheel just over a quarter-turn. At the very same moment he hit the emergency brake and engaged the clutch.

The Impala spun.

Ninety degrees into the spin, he released the brake, straightened the wheel and hit the gas, let the clutch out.

Now he faced back towards the oncoming car.

Accelerating to thirty, as he came abreast—cop's head swiveling to follow, incredulous—he hauled the wheel to the left hard and fast. Dropped into low, hit the gas, righted the wheel.

Now he was behind his pursuer.

Driver resumed speed and, clocking exactly twenty mph over, struck the cop car scant inches to the right of the left tail light. The car went skidding out of control, nose gone from north to northeast when wheels came back online and took the car the way it was headed—off the road.

To everyone's surprise, the stunt went down without a hitch, first take. The director shouted *Yes!* when the two of them climbed out of their cars. Scattered applause from cameramen, onlookers, gofers, set-up men, hangers-on.

"Righteous work out there," Driver said.

He'd driven with this guy once or twice before. Patrick something. Round Irish moonface, harelip poorly repaired, shock of unruly straw-colored hair. Belying the ethnic stereotype, a man of few words.

"Yourself," he said.

◇◇◇

Dinner that night at a restaurant out in Culver City, place packed to bursting with ponderous Mission furniture, plaster shields and tin swords on the wall, red carpeting, a front door like something you'd see on movie castles. Everything new and made up to look old. Wooden tables and chairs distressed, ceiling beams etched with acid, concrete floor ground down by polishers, cracks laid in. Thing is, the food was great. You'd swear two or three generations of women were back in the kitchen slapping out tortillas by hand, squatting by fires to roast peppers and chicken.

For all he knew, maybe they were. Sometimes he worried about that.

Driver had a few drinks in the bar first. Everything there shamelessly new, stainless steel, polished wood, as though to refute what lay outside the bat-wing doors. Halfway into his first beer he found himself in a political discussion with the man sitting next to him.

Knowing nothing of current affairs, Driver made it up as he went along. Apparently the country was about to go to war. Words such as *freedom, liberation* and *democracy* surfaced repeatedly in his companion's patter, causing Driver to remember ads for Thanksgiving turkeys, how simple it's become: just stick them in the oven and these little flags pop up to let you know they were done.

Causing Driver also to remember a man from his youth.

Every day Sammy drove his mule cart through the neighborhood crying out *Goods for sale! Goods for sale!* His cart was piled high with things no one had need of, things no one wanted. Chairs with three legs, threadbare clothing, lava lamps, fondue sets and fishbowls,

National Geographics. Day after day, year after year, Sammy went on. Why and how, no one knew.

"Can I cut in?"

Driver looked to his left.

"Double vodka, straight up," Standard told the barkeep. He took his drink to a table near the back, beckoning Driver to follow.

"Haven't seen you around much lately."

Driver shrugged. "Working."

"Any chance you'd be available tomorrow?"

"Could be."

"I've got something lined up. One of those check-cashing places. Way off the beaten path—off *any* path. Nothing around at all. Gets its bankroll for the week—and for the weekend—tomorrow before opening."

"And you know this how?"

"Let's just say, someone I met. Someone lonely. Way it looks, we're in and out in five, six minutes tops. Half an hour later you're sitting over a lunch of prime rib."

"Okay," Driver said.

"You have a vehicle?"

"I will have. The night's still young." On one hand, he didn't like so short a lead. On the other, he'd had his eye on a Buick LeSabre in the next apartment complex. Didn't look like much, but the engine sang.

"Done, then." They set a meet time and rendezvous point. "Buy you dinner?"

"I'm easy."

Both of them had steaks smothered in a slurry of onion, peppers and tomato, sides of black beans, pimento-studded rice, flour tortillas. Beer or two with dinner, then back to the bar after. TV'd been turned on but blessedly you couldn't hear it. Some brainless comedy where actors with perfect white teeth spoke their lines then froze in place to let the laugh track unwind.

Driver and Standard sat quietly together, proud men who would forever keep their own counsel. No need, use or call for banter between them.

"Rina thinks the world of you," Standard said after ordering a final round. "And Benicio loves you. You know that, right?"

"Both sentiments are fully returned."

"Any other man got that close to my woman, I'd have cut his throat long ago."

"She's not your woman."

Drinks arrived. Standard paid, adding an oversize tip. Connections everywhere, Driver thought. He identifies with these servers, knows the map of their world. A certain tenderness.

"Rina's always claimed that I expect too little from life," Standard said.

"Then at least you'll never be disappointed."

"There is that."

Clicking glasses with Driver, he drank, pulling lips back against teeth at the stringent burn of it.

"But she's right. How can I expect more than what I see here in front of me? How can any of us?" He finished his drink. "Guess we oughta be going. Get our beauty rest. Busy day tomorrow and all that."

Outside, Standard glanced up at the full moon, looked across at couples hanging out by cars, at four or five kids in gangsta finery—low-slung pants, oversize tops, head wraps—on the corner.

"Say something happened to me…" he said.

"Say it did."

"Think you might see your way clear to taking care of Irina and Benicio?"

"Yeah…Yeah, I'd do that."

"Good." They'd reached their cars by then. Uncharacteristically, Standard held out a hand. "See you tomorrow, my friend. Take care."

They shook.

Bouncy accordion on the Mexican station as Driver fired up his car. Back to the current apartment. Never thought of any of them as home really, however long he stayed in them. He cranked up the sound.

Happy music.

Before he could pull out, two firetrucks came screaming down the street, followed by an ancient sky-blue Chevy station wagon with five or six brown faces peering out from within, coop of chickens lashed to the top.

Life.

Chapter Sixteen

Nothing in the Chevy to lead him anywhere. An empty container, essentially. Impersonal as a carry cup. He'd have been surprised if it were otherwise.

If he had some way to run the registration, nine to one it was bogus. And even if it wasn't, all it was going to tell him was the car'd been stolen.

Okay.

But the hand had been dealt. He was holding.

When their hard boys didn't come back—the fat man, the albino—those who sent them would be sending someone in after. Too many loose ends whipping about in the wind, only a matter of time before someone got whacked in the head.

That was the advantage he had.

Driver figured the best thing he could do was move the Chevy. Stow it where it would be hard but not too hard to find. Then hang close by and wait.

So for two days, arm aching like a son of a bitch the whole time, figurative knives slitting shoulder to wrist again and again, ghost axe poised and descending whenever he moved, Driver sat across from the mall where he'd parked the Chevy. He forced himself to use the bad arm, even for the chi-chi coffee he bought, $3.68 a cup, at an open stall just inside the mall's east entrance. This was in Scottsdale, back towards Phoenix proper, a high-end suburb where each community had its own system of walls, where malls teeter-tottered on a Neiman-Marcus, Williams-Sonoma axis. Sort of place a vintage car like the Chevy wouldn't seem too far out of place, actually, there among the Mercedes and Beemers. Driver had parked it on the lot's outer edge in the sketchy shade of a couple of palo verdes to make it easier to spot.

Not that it much mattered at this point, but he kept running the script in his head.

Cook had set them all up, of course. Little doubt about that. Driver'd seen Strong go down—for good, to every appearance. Maybe Strong had been part of the set-up, maybe like the rest of them only a board piece, a shill, a beard. Blanche he wasn't sure about. She could have been in from the first, but it didn't feel that way. Could be she was only looking out for herself, keeping her options open, trying to find some way out of the corner she and Driver had been shoehorned into. Far as Driver knew, Cook was still a player. No way Cook had the weight or stones for those hard boys come to collect, though. So he had to be fronting.

Making the question: Who was likely to show?

Any minute a car could pull up with goombahs inside.

Or maybe, just maybe, the bosses would quietly suggest, the way it sometimes worked, that Cook clean up after himself.

Nine-forty a.m. on the third day, every breeze in the state gone severely south and blacktop already blistering, arm hanging from his shoulder like a hot anvil, Driver thought: *Okay then, Plan B*, as he watched Cook in a Crown Vic circle twice on the outer ring and pull into the lot just past the Chevy. Watched him get out, look around, amble toward the parked car with key in hand.

Cook opened the driver-side door, slid in. Soon he emerged, went around back and popped the trunk. Half his body disappeared beneath the lid.

"Shotgun's not much good anymore," Driver said.

Cook's head banged against the trunk as he tried to straighten and turn at the same time.

"Sorry about that. Blanche isn't much good either. But I thought a few props might put you in a nostalgic mood, help you remember what went down. Show and tell."

Cook's hand rose towards the hoop in his right ear. Driver intercepted it halfway and struck with one knuckle just above the wrist, at a nerve center that shut down sensation and scrambled incoming messages. He'd picked that up on breaks from a stunt man he'd worked with on a Jackie Chan movie. Then, just like a dance step, right foot forward, slide the left, pivot on the heels, he had Cook in a choke hold. Same stuntman taught him that.

"Hey, relax. Guy I learned this from told me the hold's absolutely safe on a short-term basis," he said. "After four minutes, the brain starts shutting down, but up till then—"

Loosening his hold, he let Cook drop to the ground. Man's tongue was extended and he didn't seem to be breathing. M.E. would call the skin tone blue, but it was really gray. Tiny stars of burst blood vessels about the face.

"Always a chance I didn't get it quite right, of course. Been a while, after all."

Shafts of pain shot along Driver's arm as he fished out Cook's wallet. Nothing much of use or note there.

Check the chariot, then.

In the Crown Vic he found a clutch of gas-station receipts jammed into the glove compartment, all of them from the downtown area, Seventh Street, McDowell, Central. Four or five pages of scrawled directions, mostly unreadable, to various spots in and around Phoenix. Half a torn ticket from something called Paco Paco, a matchbook from "a gentleman's cabaret," Philthy Phil's. An Arizona roadmap. And a sheaf of coupons bound together with crossed rubber bands.

NINO'S PIZZA
(RESTAURANT IN BACK)
719 E. Lynwood
(480) 258-1433
WE DELIVER

Chapter Seventeen

He always had his first few drinks of the day away from
the house. There were two choices, Rosie's up on Main,
a long haul without a car, or The Rusty Nail at the
corner. He had a car but the driver's license had gone
south years ago and he didn't like to take unwarranted
chances. Rosie's was a workingman's bar, open at six
a.m. You asked for bourbon or whisky here, the barkeep
didn't have to come back with what flavor, there was
only one bottle of each. Man didn't have to put up
with troublesome things like windows, either, since the
place was a cave. The Rusty Nail, basically a titty bar,
opened at nine. From then till three or so, when the
girls started straggling in and the clientele changed (he'd
got caught unaware more than once), it was inhabited
by mechanics from a truck garage down the street and
butchers from the meat-packing house directly across,
many of them wearing their blood-spotted aprons. So

mostly, those days his legs weren't too wobbly or his shakes too bad anyway, Rosie's won out.

All the early morning drinkers were regulars, but no one spoke. Most days the door was propped open with a chair, and whenever someone came through it, heads would swivel that way and occasionally one or another nodded a silent greeting before returning to his drink. Benny would have a double waiting by the time he reached the bar. Missed you yesterday, he might say. Benny'd serve up the first couple of drinks in a highball glass—till his hands steadied. This morning he was later than usual. Bad night? Benny asked. Couldn't sleep. My old man always blamed that on a bad conscience, Benny said. Well there you go, *he* figures it's a bad conscience, I'm thinking it's got a lot more to do with a bad chicken-fried steak.

Someone tapped his shoulder.

"Doc? You're Doc, aren't you?"

Ignore him.

"Of course you are. Buy you a drink?"

Maybe not ignore him.

Benny brings the guy another Bud and pours another double for Doc.

"Thing is, I know you, man. I'm from Tucson. You used to take care of the vatos from the racetrack. Few years back, you patched up my brother after a bank job. Noel Guzman? Wiry and tall? Bleached hair?"

No way he remembered. He'd treated dozens of them in his day. *Back in the day*, as they said now—and found himself wondering again where that came from. *Back in the day. Up in here.* You'd never heard these phrases before, then suddenly everyone was using them.

"I don't do that anymore."

"Neither does my brother, now that he's dead."

Doc threw back his scotch. "I'm sorry."

"He wasn't much, mind you—just family."

Benny was there with the bottle. Be hard for the young man to do other than approve a pour. He watched with something akin to horror as the six-dollar charge came up on the register, then with a shake of his head accepted it. Benny tucked the tab under an ashtray on the bar by them.

"Went down trying to knock off some gook mom-and-pop store. Little guy was over the counter before he knew it, the police said, had him on the floor half a second later, blood supply to his brain shut off. Not the end he imagined for himself."

"When's it ever?"

"Not that anyone else was surprised." He drained his beer and obviously wanted another. Hesitant because that might imply another six-dollar scotch as well.

"This round's on me," Doc told him. Benny took away the highball glass and set a shot glass before him, poured. Doc's hand was steady as he lifted it.

"Same?" Benny asked the kid.

"Whatever you want," Doc said.

"Bud's good."

Benny brought him a can. Doc bumped his empty shot glass against it and the kid drank.

"So…You living up this way now?"

Doc nodded.

"Doing what?"

"Retired."

"Man, you were retired when I first met you."

Shrugging, Doc signaled for a drink. Got a little extra in this one, since it was the end of a bottle. It reminded Doc of Sterno. Once as a kid he'd gone out behind the house, into the wilds of pecan trees and hedges and, following a night zipped into an army-surplus unsleeping bag, had attempted to fry bacon over a Sterno can, managing only to cook his thumb.

"Thing is, I have this sweet deal."

Of course he did. Guys like this, came up to you at a bar, knew you or claimed to, they always had a sweet deal, wanted to tell you about it.

"Not following in your brother's footsteps, I hope."

"Hey, you know how it is. Some families turn out doctors, some produce lawyers…."

The kid took off his shoe, pulled back the insole and fished out two hundred-dollar bills, which he laid on the bar. Part of the stash he'd use to make bail, as proof against vagrancy charges, for bribes, or just to get by—an old convict's habit.

Doc glanced at the bills.

"What's your name, boy?"

"Eric. Eric Guzman. Think of that as on-call pay."

"You expecting to need medical care soon?"

"Nah, not me. I'm careful. Plan ahead."

What the hell, maybe this kid's whole life was a non sequitur. Beer couldn't have hit him that hard. Not Bud, and not in the couple hours he'd been sucking at it. Doc looked up and saw the kid's pinpoint pupils. Okay. Now it makes sense.

"Planning ahead's what I'm doing. Something *does* happen, I'll know where to come, right?"

Kid didn't know shit. None of them did these days. Fancied themselves outlaws, every one of them. Up in society's face, down for anything that went counter.

Doc suffered another half-hour of Eric Guzman before making excuses and hauling his own sorry ass off the barstool and back home. Long enough for Guzman to tell him about his sweet deal. They were taking out an electronics store on Central, but way out at city's edge where the street kind of petered out, with mainly warehouses and the like around. Place was having a blow-out weekend sale, and Guzman figured by Sunday there was going to be one hell of a pile of money on hand. Security guards were all about a hundred and ten. Had his crew together, all they needed now was a driver.

Miss Dickinson was waiting for Doc, complaining, when he came up the driveway. She'd wandered in his door a year or so back when he'd had it open late one afternoon, and he'd been feeding her ever since. A mixed breed in which Russian Blue was most evident, she was missing half her left ear and two toes on the left front foot.

"How many meals is this today, Miss D?" he asked. There was a troubling regularity to her visits; he suspected she made rounds from house to house all over the neighborhood. But he opened a can of albacore tuna and set it in a corner where she could get to it and didn't have to chase it all about the room, though she would anyway, long after it was empty.

He hadn't cleaned up from the night before. Strips of blood-soaked cloth, four-by-fours, bowls of peroxide and Betadine. Bleach, stainless steel sewing needles, bottles of alcohol.

Good to be useful again.

Before he finished the clean-up, Miss Dickinson downed the tuna and came over to see what he was doing, wrinkling her nose at bleach and cleansers, steering wide of peroxide and Betadine, but showing great interest in blood-soaked cloth, cotton and gauze. She kept trying to paw these out of the serving bowls and plastic bins into which he'd tossed them.

His new patient was coming back for a check-up on Friday. Worried about infection, Doc had told him. Now he was wondering if infection was the lesser danger. He should warn his patient about Eric Guzman.

Chapter Eighteen

For a long time after Standard's death he didn't take on any more jobs. Not that he wasn't approached. Word gets around. He watched a lot of TV with Benicio, cooked huge meals for and with Irina. "Learned out of self defense," he'd said when she asked how he'd found his way to cooking. Then, as he grated fresh Parmesan, Italian sausages laid out on the cutting board to warm, he told her about his mother. They clicked glasses. A good, inexpensive sauvignon blanc.

Day or two a week, he'd go off to the studio, give them what they wanted, be back before Benicio got home from school. The checks Jimmie sent him each month grew. He could go on like this forever. Nothing gold can stay—he remembered that from a poem he'd read back in high school.

Not that in L.A. you could easily tell without consulting a calendar, but fall had arrived. Nights were cool and breezy. Each evening, light flattened itself against the horizon trying heroically to hold on, then was gone.

Home from her new job as ward clerk at the local ER, Irina refilled their wineglasses.

"Here's to—"

He remembered the glass falling, shattering as it struck the floor.

He remembered the starburst of blood on her forehead, the snail of it down her cheek as she tried to spit out what was in there in the moment before she collapsed.

He remembered catching her as she fell—and then, for a long time, not much else.

Gang business, the police would tell him later. Some sort of territorial dispute, we think.

Irina died just after four a.m.

Driver having no legal rights, Benicio got shipped off to grandparents in Mexico City. For a year or more he'd write the boy every week, and Benicio would send back drawings. He'd put them up on the refrigerator of whatever apartment he was living in, if it had a refrigerator. For a while there he kept on the hop, moving cribs every month or two, old Hollywood to Echo Park to Silverlake, thinking that might help. Time went by, which is what time does, what it is. Then one day it came to him how long it had been since he'd heard from the boy. He tried calling, but the number was out of service.

Hating to be alone, to face empty apartments and the day's gapping hours, Driver kept busy. Took everything that came his way and went looking for more. Even had a speaking part in one movie when, half an hour into the shoot, a bit player grew ill.

The director ran it down for him.

"You pull in and this guy's standing there. You shake your head, like you're feeling sorry for him, this poor sonofabitch, and you get out of the car, leaning back against the door. 'Your call,' you tell him. Got it?"

Driver nodded.

"That just goddamn *dripped* with menace," the director said later when they broke for lunch. "Two words—just two fucking words! It was beautiful. You should think seriously about doing more."

He did, but not the way the director meant.

Standard used to hang out a lot at a bar called Buffalo Diner just off Broadway in downtown L.A. Food hadn't been served there since Nixon's reign, but the name survived, as did, in patches, the chalk in which the last menu had been put up on a blackboard above the bar. So Driver started being there afternoons. Strike up conversations, stand a few drinks, mention he was a friend of Standard's, ask if they knew anyone looking for a first-rate driver. By the second week he'd become a regular, knew the rest of them by name, and had more work than he could handle.

Meanwhile, as he began turning down shoots, and went on turning them down, offers declined.

"What am I supposed to tell these people?" Jimmie said the first few times.

Within weeks he shifted to: "They want the best. That's what they keep telling me." Even the Italian guy with all the forehead creases and warts had been calling, he said—in person, not just through some secretary or handler. In goddamn person.

"Look," Jimmie's penultimate message said. By this time Driver had stopped answering the phone. "I have to figure you're alive but I'm starting not to give half a goddamn, if you know what I mean. What I'm telling people is I seem to have acquired a second asshole."

His last message said: "Been fun, kid, but I just lost your number."

Chapter Nineteen

From a phone booth Driver called the number on the coupons. The phone rang and rang at the other end—after all, it was still early. Whoever finally answered was adamant, as adamant as one could be in dodgy English, that Nino's was not open and please he would have to call back after eleven please.

"I could do that," Driver said, "but it's possible your boss won't be happy when he finds you've kept him waiting."

Too big a mouthful, apparently.

"It's also possible that you could pass me along to someone whose English is a tad better."

A homeless man went by on the street outside pushing a shopping cart piled high. Driver thought again of Sammy and his mule cart laden with things no one wanted.

A new voice came on. "Can I be of service, sir?"

"I hope so. Seems I find myself in possession of something that's not mine."

"And that would be…?"

"Close to a quarter of a million dollars."

"Please hold, sir."

Within moments a heavy, chesty voice came on the line.

"Nino here. Who the fuck's there. Dino says you have something of mine?"

Nino and Dino? "So I have reason to believe."

"Yeah, well, lots of people have stuff of mine. I got a lot of stuff. What was your name again?"

"I'd just as soon keep it. I've had it a long time."

"Why the hell not? I don't need no more names either." He turned away. "I'm on the fuckin' phone here, you can't see that?" Then back: "So what's the deal?"

"Recently I had some business with a man from out your way driving a Crown Vic."

"It's a popular car."

"It is. What I wanted to let you know is that he won't be doing any more business. Nor will Strong and Blanche. Or two gentlemen who checked out for the last time, though it wasn't their room, at a Motel 6 north of Phoenix."

"Phoenix is a hard town."

Driver could hear the man breathing there at the end of the line.

"What are you, some kind of fuckin' army?"

"I drive. That's what I do. All I do."

"Yeah. Well, I've gotta tell you, it's sounding to me like sometimes you give a little extra value for the money, if you know what I mean."

"We're professionals. People make deals, they need to stick to them. That's the way it works, if it's going to work at all."

"My old man used to say the same thing."

"I haven't counted, but Blanche told me there's something over two hundred grand in the bag."

"There damn well better be. And you're telling me this because?"

"Because it's your money and your bag. Say the word, both can be at your door within the hour."

Driver heard something fizzy and sinuous, Sinatra maybe, playing in the background.

"You're not very good at this, are you?"

"At what I do, I'm the best. This isn't what I do."

"I can go with that. So what do you get out of it?"

"Just that: out of it. Once the money's in your hands, we're even. You forget Cook and his Crown Vic, forget the goons at that Motel 6, forget we've ever had this conversation. No one steps up to me a week from now, or a month from now, with your regards."

Silence beat its way down the line. Music started up again at the far end.

"What if I refuse?" Nino said.

"Why would you? You have nothing to lose and a quarter of a million to gain."

"Good point."

"We have a deal, then?"

"We have a deal. Within the hour…?"

"Right. Just remember what your old man said."

Chapter Twenty

Doc threw sponges, swabs, syringes and gloves into a plastic bucket produced to fit against floorboards and serve as a wastebasket for cars. Hey, he lived in a garage, right? Lived on an island, he'd use coconut shells. No problem.

"That's it," he said. "Stitches are out, the wound looks good."

Bad news was that his patient wasn't going to have a whole lot of feeling in that arm from now on.

Good news was, he had full mobility.

Driver handed over a wad of bills secured with a rubber band.

"Here's what I figure I owe you. That's not enough—"

"I'm sure it is."

"Not the first time you stapled my ass back together, after all."

"1950 Ford, wasn't it?"

"Like the one Mitchum drove in *Thunder Road*, yeah."

That was really a '51—you could tell by the V-8 emblems, *Ford Custom* on front fenders, dashboard and steering wheel—but chrome windsplits had been removed and a '50 grille added. Close enough.

"You crashed into the supports of the freeway approach that had just gone up."

"Forgot it was there. It hadn't been, the last few times I made that run."

"Perfectly understandable."

"Something wonky about the car, too."

"Might cause a man to take caution who he steals a car from."

"*Borrows* a car from. I was going to take it back.... Seriously, Doc: You had my back then and you have it now. Appreciate the heads-up on Guzman. I saw the news. All three of them went down at the scene."

"Figures. He was basically your purest brand of trouble."

"Not many that'd crew up with a one-armed driver. I was desperate, I'd have taken on just about anything at that point. You knew that."

But Doc had drifted off into his own world, as he did sometimes, and made no response.

Miss Dickinson rushed up, front legs stiff and hitting ground together, then the back, like a rocking horse, as Driver was leaving. Doc had told him about her. He let her in and closed the door. Last he saw, she was sitting quietly at Doc's feet, waiting.

Doc was thinking about a story he'd read by Theodore Sturgeon. This guy, not playing with a full deck, lives in a garage apartment like his. He's brutish, elemental; much of life escapes him. But he can fix anything. One day he finds a woman in the street. She's been beaten, all but killed. He takes her back to the apartment and—Sturgeon goes into great detail about provisions for blood drainage, makeshift surgical instruments, the moment-to-moment practicalities—repairs her.

What was it called?

"Bright Segment"—that's it.

If in our lives we have one or two of those, one or two bright segments, Doc thought, we're fortunate. Most don't.

And the rest wasn't silence, like that opera, *I Pagliacci*, said.

The rest was just noise.

Chapter Twenty-one

Best job Driver ever had was a remake of *Thunder Road*. Hell, two-thirds of the movie was driving. That '56 Chevy, with Driver inside, was the real star.

The production was one of those things that just fell together out of nowhere, two guys sitting in a bar talking favorite movies. They were brothers, and had had a couple of minor money-makers aimed at the teen market. Both pretty much geeks, but good enough guys. The older one, George, was the front man, took care of the production end, finding money, all that. His younger brother, Junie, did most of the directing. They wrote the films together during all-nighters at various Denny's in central L.A.

They'd been running scenes and lines from *Thunder Road* for three or four minutes when they both got quiet at the same time.

"We could do it," George said.

"We could for damn sure try."

By the next day's end, with nothing on paper, no treatment, not a single word of script, nary a spreadsheet or projection in sight, they had it together. Contingent commitments from investors, a distributor, the whole nine yards. Their lawyer was looking into rights and permissions.

What tipped it was, they approached the hottest young actor of the year, who turned out to be a huge fan of Robert Mitchum. "Man I wanted to *be* Bob Mitchum!" he said, and signed on. Driver had worked on the movie that made him a star. He was a little shit even then and hadn't got any better. Lasted another year or two before he dropped off the face of the earth. You'd hear about him from time to time in the tabloids after that. He'd gone into rehab again, he was poised for a comeback, he was set for a guest spot on some lame sitcom. But right then he was hot property, and with him on board, everything else fell into place.

What a lot of people don't know about the original is how that Ford used in the crash scene had to be specially built. They put on cast-steel front bumpers, heavily reinforced the body and frame, modified the engine for maximum horsepower, then realized that no regular tires could handle the weight and speed and had to have those specially made as well, of solid sponge rubber. All the moonshiner cars in the movie were real. They'd been employed by moonshiners in the Asheville, North Carolina, area who sold them to the film company then used the money to buy newer, faster cars.

Driver was principal on the film, with a young guy out of Gary, Indiana, Gordon Ligocki, doing most of the rest. He had a duck's ass right out of the Fifties, wore an I.D. bracelet that had *Your Name* engraved on it, and spoke so softly you had to ask him to repeat half of what he said.

"( )," he said that first day as they took a lunch break.

"Sorry?" Driver said.

"Said you drive well."

"You too."

They sat quietly. Ligocki was tossing back cans of Coke. As Driver ate his sandwiches and fruit and sipped coffee, he was thinking how if he did that, he'd be calling time out halfway through every stunt to pee.

"( )."

"What?"

"Said you got family?"

"No, just me."

"Been out here long?"

"Few years. You?"

"Close on to a year now. Hard to get to know anyone in this town. People'll talk to you at the drop of a hat, just never seems to go much beyond that."

Although over the next year or two they'd spend time in one another's company, having the occasional meal together, going out for drinks, that was the longest string of words Driver ever knew Ligocki to put together. Whole evenings could go by with not much at all between "How's it going" and "Next time," something they were both comfortable with.

That movie was the hardest Driver ever worked on. It was also the most fun he'd ever had. One stunt in particular took him most of a day to get down. He was to come barreling along the street, see a roadblock, and go for a wall. Had to take the car almost completely sideways without turning over, so the speed and angle had to be perfect. First couple of run-throughs, he rolled. Third time he thought he had it, but the director told him afterwards that there was some sort of technical problem and they'd have to run it again. Four tries later, he nailed it.

Driver didn't know what happened, but the movie never got released. Something about rights maybe, or some other legal issue, could be any one of a hundred problems. Most things that start out to be movies don't ever get made. They'd had this one in the can, though, and it was good.

Go figure.

Chapter Twenty-two

Six a.m., first light of dawn, world stitching itself back together out there, reconstituting itself, as he looked on.

Blink, and the warehouse across the way reemerged.

Blink again, the city loomed in the distance, a ship coming hard into port.

Birds skittered from ragged tree to ragged tree complaining. Cars idled at curbside, took on human freight, pulled away.

Driver sat in his apartment sipping scotch from the only glass he'd kept. The scotch was Buchanan's, a mid-range blend. Not bad at all. Big seller among Latinos. No phone service here, nothing of value. Couch, bed and chairs came with the rent. Clothes, razor, money and other essentials waited in a duffel bag by the door.

Just as a good car waited in the parking lot.

The TV, he'd found sitting beside garbage bags at curbside when he put out his own glasses, dishes and miscellaneous goods for pickup. *Why not?* he thought. Ten-inch screen, and pretty much banged to hell, but it worked. So now he was watching a nature program in which four or five coyotes chased a jackrabbit. The dogs were relaying: one would chase the rabbit a while, then another would take over.

Sooner or later they'd come after him, of course. Only a matter of time. Nino'd known that all along. They both had. The rest was no more than dancing, fancy footwork and misdirection, figure-eight of the bullfighter's cape. No way they were going to just let this lie.

Driver poured the last of the Buchanan's into his last glass.

Guests soon, no doubt about it.

Chapter Twenty-three

In his dream the jackrabbit stopped dead still and turned on the coyote, curling its lips back to reveal huge razor-sharp teeth just before it sprang.

That's when Driver woke and knew someone was in the room. A change in the quality of darkness at the window told him where the intruder was. Driver turned heavily in bed, as though restless, bed frame banging against the wall.

The man stopped moving.

Driver turned again and kept going, springing onto his feet. The radio antenna in his hand slashed at the man's neck. There was much blood, and for a moment, two beats, three, the man stood as if frozen. By then Driver was behind him. He kicked the man's legs out from under and, as he went down, slashed again with the antenna, at the other side this time, then at the hand that was reaching for, presumably, a gun.

Bending down, foot planted on the man's arm, Driver pulled it out. A short-barrelled .38. As though the poor little thing had had a nose job to help it fit in.

"Okay. On your feet."

"Whatever you say." His visitor held up both hands, palm out. "I'm cool."

Hardly more than a kid, really. Bulked up from workouts and steroids in equal measure. Dark hair cut almost to the scalp on the sides, left long on top. Sport coat over a black T-shirt, couple of gold chains. Small, square teeth. Not like the jackrabbit's at all.

Driver urged him through the front door and out onto the balcony that circled the building. All the apartments opened onto it.

"Jump," Driver said.

"You're crazy, man. We're on the second floor."

"Your call. I don't much care either way. Either you jump or I shoot you where you stand. Think about it. It's only what, thirty feet or so? You'll live through it. Any luck at all, you get off with only a couple broken legs, maybe a shattered ankle."

Driver marked the moment it changed, saw the moment when the tension went away and his body accepted what was about to happen. The man put one hand on the railing.

"Give my regards to Nino," Driver said.

Afterwards he collected the duffel bag from inside the door and went down the back stairs to his car.

Jumpin' Jack Flash came on the radio when the engine caught.

Shit.

Obviously the station had, as they liked to say, changed its profile. Bought out? Sold down the river? Supposed to be soft jazz, damn it. Still was, just days ago, when he set the buttons. Now this.

Getting to be where you can't rely on anything.

Driver spun the dial through country music, news, a talk show about aliens of the extraterrestrial sort, easy listening, country again, hard rock, another talk show about aliens of the earthbound sort, news again.

Concerned citizens of Arizona were up in arms because a humanitarian group had begun installing water stations in the desert that illegal immigrants had to cross to get from Mexico to the U.S. Thousands had perished trying to make the crossing. *Concerned citizens of Arizona*, Driver noted, came out all in a breath, like *weapons of mass destruction* or *the red threat*.

Meanwhile the state legislature was trying to pass statutes barring illegal aliens from free medical care in Arizona's overburdened, uncompensated emergency rooms and hospitals.

Doc should start up a franchise.

Driver pulled onto the interstate.

They'd sent a single dog after him? And a new dog to boot, not even pick of the litter. That was plain stupid, made no sense whatsoever.

Or maybe it did.

Two possibilities.

One: they were trying to set him up. His designated assassin wouldn't talk, of course. But if Driver had killed him—as whoever sent him had every reason to expect—police even now would be going door to door and checking apartment-house records. All over California and adjoining states, fax machines would be rousing from slumber to spit out stats of the photo from Driver's old DMV records and whatever other information about him could be unearthed. There wasn't a lot; even back then, instinctively, he kept his head down.

The second possibility hardened to reality when a blue Mustang came up around the chain of cars behind him outside Sherman Oaks, lodged in his rear view mirror, and wouldn't be shaken.

So not only did they have a tail on him, they wanted him to *know* they had a tail on him.

Driver cut abruptly off the interstate and into a service area, bypassing the inner loop. Pulled in and sat, engine purring, out by the truckers. Nearby, a family spilled from its van with dogs in tow, parents shouting at kids, kids shouting at dogs and one another.

The Mustang materialized behind him, in his mirror.

Okay then, he thought. *My game now.*

Popping the clutch, he shot along the service road. As he gained speed, his eyes swept constantly from rear view mirror to highway and back again. With a car length to spare, he slid onto the highway between two semis.

But he couldn't lose the son of a bitch whatever he tried.

Periodically he'd go off-road, blend into local traffic to take advantage of it, interpose traffic lights like blockades between himself and his pursuer. Or back on the interstate he'd accelerate with blinkers going as though to take the off ramp, drop in front of a rig, then, once out of sight, floor it and surge ahead.

Whatever he did, the Mustang hung there behind like a bad memory, history you can't escape.

Desperate times, desperate measures.

Well out of the city, out where the first of a crop of white windmills, lazily turning, wound sky down to desert, Driver sailed without warning onto an exit ramp and into a one-eighty. Sat facing back the way he'd come as the Mustang raced towards him.

Then he hit the gas.

He was out for a minute or two, no more. An old stunt man's trick: at the last moment, he'd thrown himself into the back seat and braced for the collision.

The cars struck head-on. Neither was going to leave on its own steam, but the Mustang, predictably, got the worst of it. Kicking his door open, Driver climbed out.

"You okay?" someone shouted from the window of a battered pickup idling at the bottom of the off ramp.

Then the long blare of a horn and a squeal of brakes as a Chevy van skidded to a stop, rocking, behind the pickup.

Driver stepped up to the Mustang. Sirens in the distance.

Gordon Ligocki's ducktail would never look good again. His neck was broken. Internal damages too, judging from the blood around his mouth. Probably slammed into the steering wheel.

Driver still had the coupons for Nino's Pizza.

He tucked one into Gordon Ligocki's shirt pocket.

Chapter Twenty-four

He hitched a ride with the guy in the pickup, whose emergence with an aluminum baseball bat had sufficiently adjusted attitudes among the youthful crew of the van as to send them spinning away into traffic.

"What I'm guessing is you may have good reason not to be around once the Man arrives," he said when Driver approached him. "Know more than a little about that myself. Get on up here."

Driver climbed aboard.

"Name's Jodie," he said a mile or so down the road, "but nearabouts everyone calls me Sailor." He pointed to a tattoo on his right bicep. "Supposed to be a bat wing. Looks like a mainsail."

Professionally done tattoos—the bat, a woman in a grass skirt with coconut shells for breasts, an American flag, a dragon—covered his biceps. Hands on the steering wheel bore another sort of tattoo. Jailhouse tattoos, crudely done with ink and the end of a wire. Most times, that meant a guitar string.

"Where're we headed?" Driver asked.

"Depends....Town not far up the road has a decent enough dinner. You hungry by any chance?"

"I could eat."

"How did I know?"

It was a classic small-town noontime buffet, steam trays piled high with slices of meat loaf, shrimp, hot wings, beans and franks, home fries, roast beef. Sides of cottage cheese, three-layer Jell-O salad, green salad, pudding, carrot and celery sticks, green bean casserole. Clientele a mix of blue-collar workers, men and women from offices nearby in short-sleeve dress shirts and polyester dresses, blue-haired old ladies. These last came out in their tank-like cars around one o'clock each afternoon, Jodie told him, heads barely visible above steering wheel and dash. Everyone else knew to get off the streets then.

"You don't have work you need to be tending to?" Driver asked.

"Nope, time's my own. Have Nam to thank for that. I'm up for armed robbery, see, and the judge says he'll give me a choice, I can enlist or I can go back to prison. Didn't much care for it the first time round, didn't have any notion it would have got much better. So I slide through basic, ship out, then along about three months in, I'm sitting there having the first of my usual breakfast beers when a sniper takes me down. Spilled the whole can. Fucker's been up there all night waiting.

"They airlift me to Saigon, take out half of one lung and pack me back Stateside. Disability's enough to get by on, long as I don't develop a taste for much more than greasy hamburgers and cheap hootch."

He threw back the rest of his coffee. The hula girl on his arm shimmied. Spare flesh like a turkey's wattles swung beneath.

"Had the feeling you might have seen action yourself."

Driver shook his head.

"Prison, then. You've been inside."

"Not yet."

"And here I'd of sworn...." He took another try at the coffee cup, registered surprise to find it empty. "What the hell do I know, anyway."

"How's the rest of your day look?" Driver said.

Like shit, apparently. And like usual. Jodie's home was a trailer in Paradise Park back towards the interstate. Abandoned refrigerators, stacks of bald tires and tireless, decaying vehicles sat everywhere. Half a dozen dogs in the compound barked and snarled nonstop. Jodie's kitchen sink would have been heaped with dishes if he'd had enough dishes to heap. Those few he had *were* in the sink, and looked to have been there for some time. Grease swam in the runnels of stove-top burners.

Jodie snapped on the TV when they first came in, rooted around in the sink, rinsed out a couple of glasses with tap water and filled them with bourbon. A scabrous dog of uncertain parentage made its way out of the back of the trailer to greet them, then, exhausted by the effort, collapsed at their feet.

"That's General Westmoreland," Jodie told him.

They sat watching an old *Thin Man* movie, then a *Rockford Files*, steadily downing bourbon. Three hours later, just before Driver rode off in his truck, leaving behind a note that read *Thank you* and a stack of fifty-dollar bills, Jodie collapsed, too. Just like the dog.

Chapter Twenty-five

It came in a box not much larger than one of the encyclopedias lined up on a shelf in the front room behind dusty figurines of fish and angels. How could such a thing fit in there? A *table?* Accent table, the ad said, crafted by one of America's premier designers, assembly required.

It arrived around noon. His mother had been so excited. We'll wait and open it after lunch, she said.

She'd ordered the table by mail. He remembered being amazed at this. Would the postman ring the bell and, when she opened the door, hand it through? Your table's here, ma'am. You draw a circle, write a number on a piece of paper and enclose a check, a table shows up at your door. That's magic enough. But it also comes in this tiny box?

Further memories of his mother, of his early life, drift up occasionally in pre-dawn hours. He wakes with them lodged in his head, but the moment he tries consciously to remember, or to express them, they're gone.

He was, what?, nine or ten years old? Sitting at the kitchen table dawdling over a peanut butter sandwich while his mother drummed fingers on the counter.

Through? she said.

He wasn't, there was still almost half a sandwich on his plate and he was hungry, but he nodded. Always agree. That was the first rule.

She swept his plate away, into a stack of others by the sink.

So let's have a look. Stabbing a butcher knife into one end of the box to rip it open.

Lovingly she laid out components on the floor. What an impossible puzzle. Lengths of cheap contoured metal and tubing, wedges of rubber, baggies of screws and fittings.

His mother's eyes kept returning to the instruction sheet as, moment by moment, piece by piece, she assembled the table. By the time feet had been fitted with rubber stoppers and the bottom half of legs were in place, the expression on her face, to which he was ever attentive, had gone from happy to puzzled. As she spliced on upper legs, cross-supports and screws, her expression turned sad. That prospect of sadness spread throughout her body, washed out into the room.

Watch closely: that's the second rule.

Mother lifted the table top out of the bottom of the box and set it in place.

An ugly, cheap-looking, wobbly thing.

The room, the world, got very quiet. Both stayed that way for a long time.

I just don't understand, Mother said.

She sat on the floor still, pliers and screwdrivers ranged about her. Tears streamed down her face.

It looked so pretty in the catalog. So pretty. Not at all like this.

Chapter Twenty-six

Jodie's former ride was a Ford F-150, graceless as a wheelbarrow, dependable as rust and taxes, indestructible as a tank. Brakes that could stop an avalanche cold, engine powerful enough to tow glaciers into place. Bombs fall and wipe out civilization as we know it, two things'll come up out of the ashes: roaches and F-150s. Thing handled like an ox cart, rattled fillings from teeth and left you permanently saddle sore, but it was a survivor. Got the job done, whatever the job was.

Like him.

Driver steered the mostly black beast with patches of Bond-It back down I-10 towards L.A. He'd found a college station playing Eddie Lang-Lonnie Johnson duets, George Barnes, Parker with Dolphy, Sidney Bechet, Django. Funny how so small a victory, finding that station, could change your whole outlook.

At a barbershop on Sunset he had his head buzzed almost to the scalp. Bought oversize clothes and wrap-around mirror shades next door.

Nino's shouldered up against a bakery and a butcher shop in an Italian neighborhood where old women sat out on porches and front steps and men played dominos at card tables set up on the sidewalk. What with supermarkets, Sam's Clubs and so on, Driver hadn't known butcher shops still existed.

Two guys in dark suits, in particular, put in a lot of time at Nino's. They'd show up early in the morning, have breakfast and sit around a while, then leave. Hour or so later, they'd be back. Sometimes that'd go on all day long. One slammed espressos, the other went with wine.

Came right down to it, they were a study in opposites.

Espresso Man was young. Late twenties maybe, black hair cut short and troweled in place with what looked for all the world like Vaseline. Shine UV on that hair, it would fluoresce. Round-toed, clumsy-looking black shoes stuck out under the cuffs of his pants. Beneath his coat he wore a navy blue polo shirt.

Wine Man, fiftyish, wore a dark dress shirt with gold cufflinks but no tie, black Reeboks, and had his grey hair pulled back into a stubby ponytail. Where his young partner walked with the deliberate, measured step, the *meatiness*, of a bodybuilder, Wine Man just kind of drifted. Like he was in moccasins, or touched down only every third or fourth step.

◇◇◇

Second day, right after breakfast, Espresso Man stepped behind the building to have a smoke. Inhaling deeply, he drew in a lungful of slow poison, exhaled, then tried to draw in another but it wouldn't come.

Something around his neck. What the fuck—*wire*? He claws at it, knowing it'll do no good. Someone behind pulling hard. And that warmth on his chest would be blood. As he struggles to look down, an ingot of bloody flesh, *his* flesh, drops onto his chest.

So this is it, he thinks, *here in a fucking alley, with shit in my pants. Goddamn.*

Driver tucks a Nino's coupon into Espresso Man's coat pocket. Earlier he's circled "We Deliver" in red ink.

◇◇◇

God *damn,* Wine Man echoed minutes later. Nino's bodyguard brought him out here after one of the cooks, emerging to empty a grease trap, tripped over Junior.

Who the hell would name their kid Junior anyway?

Boy was gone, no doubt about it. Eyes bulging, star-patterns of burst capillaries all over his face. Tongue stuck out like a meat cork.

Amazing. Boy still had a hard-on. Sometimes he'd thought that was about all there was to Junior.

"Mr. Rose?" the bodyguard said. What was this one's name? They came and went. Keith something.

Son of a *bitch*, he thought. *Son* of a bitch.

Not that he cared much for the guy, who could be a royal pain in the ass, all pumped iron, carrot juice and steroids. And enough caffeine to kill a team of horses. But goddamn it, whoever did this had brought it where it never should have come.

"Looks like the boss needs to kick it up a notch or two, Mr. Rose," Keith-something said behind him.

He stood with his wineglass in one hand, pizza coupon in the other. The circle of red ink. We deliver.

"I'd say that's already been taken care of."

Couldn't have been more than minutes. How far away could the son of a bitch have gotten? But it wasn't for now.

He drained his glass.

"Let's go tell Nino."

"He ain't gonna like it," Keith-something said.

"Who the hell does?"

◇◇◇

Bernie Rose sure as hell didn't.

"So you've sicced the hounds on this guy and the first I hear of it is when he steps up in my own backyard and takes down my partner....Good thing there ain't no union for our kind of work. That's *my* business, Nino. You damn well know it is."

Nino, who hated pasta of every kind, tucked the last of a chocolate croissant into his mouth and followed it with a mouthful of Earl Grey tea.

"We've known each other since we were what, six years old?"

Bernie Rose said nothing.

"Trust me. This was off to the side, not business as usual. Made sense to farm it out."

"Off to the side's the sort of thing gets you taken down, Nino. You know that."

"Times are changing."

"Times are for *damn* sure changing when you send amateurs out on a kill and don't even bother to let your own men know what's going on."

Bernie Rose poured another glass of wine. Still called it dago red. Nino's eyes never left him.

"Tell me."

If he'd been in films he'd have asked what the back story was. Movie folk had this vocabulary of their own. Back story, subtext, foreshadowing, carry-through. Producers who couldn't diagram a sentence to save their lives loved to talk about the "structure" of a script.

"It's complicated."

"I bet it is."

He listened while Nino laid it out for him, the mock robbery gone south, this guy who'd taken it personally, the payoff.

"You fucked up," he said.

"Big time. Believe me, I know it. I should have brought you in. We're a team."

"Not any more," Bernie Rose said.

"Bernie—"

"Shut the fuck up, Nino."

Bernie Rose poured another glass of wine, killing the bottle. Old days, they'd jam a candle into the neck, put it on one of the tables. Goddamn romantic.

"Here's how it's gonna go. I'll take this guy down, but it's on *my* dime, nothing to do with you. And once it's done, I'm out of here—just a bad memory."

"Not that easy to walk away, my friend. You're bound."

They sat unmoving, eyes locked. It was some time before Bernie Rose spoke.

"I ain't asking your fucking permission, Izzy." His use of Nino's childhood nickname, something he'd never done before in all these years, had a visible effect. "You got your money back. Be content."

"It's not about the money—"

"—it's about the principle. Right….So you're gonna do what? Write op-ed columns for the *New York Times*? Dispatch more of your amateurs?"

"They wouldn't be amateurs."

"They're *all* amateurs nowadays. All of 'em. Carbon-copy Juniors with their goddamn tattoos and cute little ear rings. But it's your call, do what you have to."

"I always do."

"Two things."

"I'm counting."

"You send people after me, anyone up the line sends people after me, best keep the loading docks open for regular deliveries."

"This the same Bernie Rose that said 'I don't ever threaten'?"

"It's not a threat. Neither is this."

"What?" Nino's eyes met his.

"You don't get a free ride for old time's sake. I look in the mirror and see someone in the back seat, next thing I see—once I've taken care of that—is you."

"Bernie, Bernie. We're friends."

"No. We're not."

◇◇◇

What to make of this? Every time you thought you had a take on it, the world thumbed its nose and shifted back to its own track, becoming again—still—unreadable. Driver found himself wishing he had Manny Gilden's opinion. Manny understood at a glance things others spent weeks puzzling out. "Intuition," he said, "it's all intuition, just a knack I have. Everyone thinks I'm smart, but I'm not. Something in me makes these connections." Driver wondered if Manny'd ever made it to New York or if, as usual, six or seven times in as many years, he'd backed out.

Wine Man came out to look at Espresso, no expression showing on his face, and went back inside. Half an hour later he floated out the door again and saddled up. A sky-blue Lexus.

Driver thought about the way he'd stood looking down, wineglass in his hand, and how he'd looked getting into the Lexus, almost weightless, and understood for the first time what Manny had been talking about.

The guy who went in and the one who came out were different people. Something happened in there to change things.

Chapter Twenty-seven

Bernie Rose and Isaiah Paolozzi grew up in Brooklyn, the old Italian section centering around Henry Street. From the roof where Bernie had spent a good portion of his teen years you could look left to the Statue of Liberty and, right, to the bridge like a huge elastic band holding two distinct worlds together. In Bernie's time, those worlds had become ever less distinct as skyrocketing rents in Manhattan drove young people across the river, and Brooklyn rents, on the teeter-totter, rose to meet the demand. Manhattan, after all, was still but minutes away by F train. In Cobble Hill, Boerum Hill and lower Park Slope, trendy restaurants catering to the new residents sat jarringly among cluttered used-furniture stores and ancient, flyblown, hole-in-the-wall bodegas.

It was a part of town where stories about the mob circulated like the latest jokes.

One of the new residents, out walking her dog, had let it crap on the sidewalk and, in a hurry to meet her date, failed to clean up after it. Unfortunately the sidewalk fronted the home of a mobster's mother. Days later the young woman came back across the river to find the dog gutted in her bathtub.

Another, circling block after block seeking a parking place, had pulled into one just vacated. "Hey, you can't park there, that's a private spot," a kid on the stoop shouted to him. "No such thing," he'd said. Next day when he hiked the eight blocks to pull his car to the other side to make room for street cleaning and so avoid a ticket, it was gone. He never saw it again.

Back around 1990, Nino'd got fed up. "This ain't my town anymore," he told Bernie. "How's California sound?" Sounded pretty good. Not much for Bernie to do here; the business ran itself. He was bone tired of old men waving him over to their dinner and domino tables to complain, tired of the slew of cousins and nephews and nieces that comprised most of Brooklyn. And he'd drunk enough espresso to last him a lifetime. Had his last cup, in fact, the day they left. Never touched it again.

Hadn't taken Nino long to pull up ties. Sold the restaurant with its red-flocked wallpaper and big-hair waitresses to one of the newcomers with plans to make it a "sushi palace." Laid off the news stand and new chi-chi coffee houses to a couple of nephews. Uncle

Lucius, urged on by wife Louise, who wanted him out of the house whatever the cost, took over the bar.

They drove cross-country in Nino's cherry and cherry-red Cadillac, pulling into truck stops a couple times a day for hamburgers and steaks, making do the rest of the time with chips, Vienna sausages, sardines, Fritos. Before this, those few times they had reason to venture into it, even Manhattan seemed a foreign country. Brooklyn was the world. Now here they were, coursing through the wilderness of America, traversing its back lots.

"Hell of a country," Nino said, "*hell* of a country. Anything's possible, anything at all."

Well, yeah. You had family, connections, money, sure it was. Little difference between this and the political machines that spat out all those Kennedys and kept the like of Mayor Daley in office. Or the ones that chocked Reagan and a couple of Bushes under the wheels of the republic while tires got changed.

"Even if it does look," Nino added—they were in Arizona by then—"like God squatted down here, farted, and lit a match to it."

Nino stole home in their new world as though he'd always been here, taking command of an array of pizza parlors, mall-based fast food concessions, bookie action, enforcement. It was just like they'd never left, Bernie thought, only now when they looked out they didn't see elevated train tracks and painted ads for restaurants on the side of buildings, they saw blue sky and palm trees.

Bernie Rose hated it all. Hated the procession of beautiful days, hated giving up seasons and rain, hated the clotted streets and highways, hated all these so-called communities, Bel Air, Brentwood, Santa Monica, insisting on sovereignty even as they drained away L.A.'s resources.

He'd never thought of himself as a political person, but hey.

Thing was, it made him a kinder man. He went out on a collection to a doublewide or a co-op some idiot had paid two mill for, that kindness went with him. He tried to understand, tried to put himself in the others' shoes. "You're going soft, boy," Uncle Ivan said—the only person back east he kept in touch with. But he wasn't. He was just seeing how some people never had half a fucking chance and never would have.

In China Belle, well into his third cup of green tea, nibbling at the edges of an egg roll too hot to eat, Bernie sat thinking about the guy who'd set sights on Nino.

"Everything all right, Mr. Rose?" his favorite waitress, Mai June, asked. ("My father owned little aside from his sense of humor, of which he was inordinately proud," she'd told him when he asked about her name.) Like everything she said, even so phatic a statement, with its lilt and rising tones, sounded like a poem or a piece of music. He assured her the food was exemplary as always. Moments later, she brought his entrée, five-flavor shrimp.

Okay. Run it down, then.

Nino out here in Wonderland had begun fancying himself some kind of goddamn producer, no longer just a good maintenance man (and he'd been one of the best), but a mover and shaker. Such unwarranted ambition was in the very water and air, and in this pounding sunlight. Like a virus, it got into you and wouldn't let go, dog of the American Dream gone dingo. So Nino'd set up the grab, or more likely had it foisted on him, then farmed it out, probably to the foister. Director put a team together, a package. Brought in the driver.

Shouldn't be too hard to step in those footprints. Not that he knew offhand who to call, but there'd be no problem getting numbers. He'd put it out that he was a mover and shaker himself, of course, one with a heavy job waiting on the runway, only before takeoff he needed the best driver to be had.

Mai June materialized beside him, refilling his tea cup, asking if he needed anything else.

"Brave shrimp," he said. "Heroic shrimp."

Bowing her head, Mai June withdrew.

◇◇◇

As Bernie Rose chomped egg rolls and five-flavor shrimp, Driver was approaching the Lexus where it sat in the empty lot next door. Thing had an onboard alarm system that hadn't been activated.

A black-and-white swung by, slowed momentarily. Driver leaned back against the hood as if it were his own ride, heard the crackle of the radio. The cruiser went on.

Driver straightened and moved to the window of the Lexus.

Steering wheel crossed with a Club—but Driver had no use for the car, and it took him less than a minute to slimjim the door. The interior was spotless. Seats clean and empty. Nothing on the floorboards. A scant handful of refuse, drink cup, tissues, ballpoint pen, tucked neatly into a leatherette pocket hanging off the dash.

Registration in the glove compartment gave him what he wanted.

Bernard Wolfe Rosenwald.

Residing at one of those woodland names out in Culver City, probably some apartment complex with a half-assed security gate.

Driver taped one of the pizza coupons to the steering wheel. He'd drawn a happy face on it.

Chapter Twenty-eight

His eyes went up, to plastic IV bags hanging on trees above the bed, six of them. Below those a battery of pumps. They'd need to be reset every hour or so. One beeped in alarm already.

"What, another goddamn visitor?"

Driver had spoken with the charge nurse, who told him there'd been no other visitors. She also told him his friend was dying.

Doc raised a hand to point shakily to the IVs.

"See I've reached the magic number."

"What?"

"Back in med school we always said you have six chest tubes, six IVs, it's all over. You got to that point, all the rest's just dancing."

"You're going to be fine."

"Fine's a town I don't even visit anymore."

"Is there anyone I can call?" Driver asked.

Doc made scribbling motions on air. There was a clipboard on the table. Driver handed it to him.

"This is an L.A. number, right?"

Doc nodded. "My daughter."

At a bank of pay phones in the lobby, Driver dialed the number.

Thank you for calling. Your call is important to us. Please leave a message.

He said that he was calling from Phoenix, that her father was seriously ill. He left the name of the hospital and his own phone number.

When he got back, a Spanish-language soap opera was playing. A handsome, shirtless young man came struggling up out of swampland, plucking leeches off well-muscled legs.

"No answer," Driver said. "I left a message."

"She won't call back."

"Maybe she will."

"Why should she?"

"Because she's your daughter?"

Doc shook his head.

"How'd you find me?"

"I went by your place. Miss Dickinson was outside, and when I opened the door she rushed in. You two had a routine. If she was there, then you should be. I started knocking on doors, asking around. A kid across the street told me paramedics had come and taken you away."

"You feed Miss Dickinson?"

"I did."

"Bitch has us all well trained."

"Is there anything I can do for you, Doc?"

His eyes went to the window. He shook his head.

"I figured you could use this," Driver said, handing him a flask. "I'll try your daughter again."

"No reason to."

"Okay if I come back to see you?"

Doc tilted the flask to drink, then lowered it.

"Won't be much reason for that, either."

Driver was almost to the door when Doc called out: "How's that arm?"

"The arm's good."

"So was I," Doc said. "So was I."

Chapter Twenty-nine

This son of a bitch was beginning to piss him off.

Bernie Rose came out of China Belle picking his teeth. He tossed the fortune cookie in the Dumpster. Even if the damn thing held the gospel truth, who in his right mind would want to know?

Ripping the coupon off his steering wheel, he balled it up and sent it after the fortune cookie.

Pizza. Right.

Bernie drove home, to Culver City, not far from the old MGM studios, now Sony-Columbia. Jesus, one hand wrapped around a hamburger, held two fingers of the other up to his head in greeting, then hit the button to open the gate. Bernie gave him a thumbs-up in reply, wondering if Jesus knew he'd just passed a good facsimile of the Boy Scout salute.

Someone had shoved over a dozen pizza ads under his door. Pizza Hut, Mother's, Papa John's, Joe's Chicago

Style, Pizza Inn, Rome Village, Hunky-Dory Quick Ital, The Pie Place. Son of a bitch probably went around pulling them off doors all over the neighborhood. On every one of them he'd circled *Free Delivery.*

Bernie poured a scotch and sank into the swayback sofa. Right alongside was a chair he'd paid over a thousand dollars for, supposed to correct all your back problems, but he couldn't stand the damn thing, felt like he was sitting in a catcher's mitt. So, though he'd had it almost a year, it still smelled like new car. The smell, he liked.

Suddenly he felt tired.

And the couple next door were at it again. He sat listening and had another scotch before he went and knocked at 2-D.

"Yeah?"

Lenny was a short, red-faced man who'd carry his baby fat with him to the grave.

"Bernie Rose, next apartment over."

"I know, I know. What's up? I'm kind of busy here."

"I heard."

His eyes changed. He tried to close the door but Bernie had reached up and grasped the edge, forearm flat against it. Guy got even more red-faced trying to shove it closed, but Bernie held it easily. Muscles on his arm stood out like cables.

After a moment he swept it open.

"What the—"

"You all right, Shonda?" Bernie asked.

She nodded without meeting his eyes. At least it hadn't gotten to the physical stage this time. Not yet.

"You can't—"

Bernie clamped a hand on his neighbor's throat.

"I'm a patient man, Lenny, not much for getting in other people's way. What I figure is, we've all got our own lives, right? And the right to be left alone. So I sit over there for almost a year now listening to what goes down in here and I keep thinking, Hey, he's a mensch, he'll work it out. You gonna work it out, Lenny?"

Bernie rocked his hand at the wrist, causing his neighbor's head to nod.

"Shonda's a good woman. You're lucky to have her, lucky she's put up with you this long. Lucky *I've* put up with you. She has good reason: she loves you. I don't have any reason at all."

Well, *that* was stupid, Bernie thought as he returned to his own apartment and poured another scotch.

It was quiet next door. The swayback couch welcomed him, as it always did.

Had he left the TV on? He didn't recall ever turning it on at all, but there it was, unspooling one of those court shows currently fashionable, Judge Somebody-or-another, judges reduced to caricature (brusque, sarcastic New Yorker, Texan with accent thick as cake icing), participants either so stupid they jumped at the chance to broadcast their stupidity nationwide or so oblivious they had no idea that's what they were doing.

Yet another thing that made Bernie tired.

He didn't know. Had he changed, or had the world changed around him? Some days he barely recognized it. Like he'd been dropped off in a spaceship and was only going through the motions, trying to fit in, doing his best imitation of someone who belonged down here. Everything had gone so cheap and gaudy and hollow. Buy a table these days, what you got was an eighth of an inch of pine pressed onto plywood. Spend $1200 for a chair, you couldn't sit in the damn thing.

Bernie'd known his share of burnouts, guys who started wondering just what it was they were doing and why any of it mattered. Mostly they disappeared not long after. Got sent up for lifetime hauls, got sloppy and killed by someone they'd braced, got taken down by their own people. Bernie didn't think he was a burnout. This driver for damn sure wasn't.

Pizza. He hated fucking pizza.

Come right down to it, though, that was pretty funny, all those pizza ads stuck under his door.

Chapter Thirty

When Driver was a kid, every night for what seemed like a year he had this same dream. He'd be up on the side of the house with his toes on the molding, where the first floor was eight feet or so off the ground since the house was built into a hill, and there'd be a bear under him. The bear would go reaching for him, he'd pull up on a window casing, and after a while, frustrated, the bear would pick a tulip or iris from the bed of them at the base of the house and eat it. Then he'd go back to scrambling for Driver. Finally the bear would pick another tulip, look thoughtful, and offer it to Driver. Driver was always reaching for the tulip when he awoke.

This was back in Tucson, when he lived with the Smiths. His best friend then was Herb Danziger. Herb was a car nut, worked on cars in his backyard and made good money at it, challenging the pay both from his father's job as security guard and his mother's as a nurse's aide. There'd always be a '48 Ford or a '55 Chevy sitting there with the hood up and half its innards laid out on a tarp on the ground nearby. Herb had one of those massive blue Chilton automobile repair manuals, but Driver never saw him look at it, not once in all those years.

Driver's first and last fight at the new school happened when the local bully came up to him on the schoolyard and told Driver he shouldn't be hanging around Jews. Driver had vaguely been aware that Herb was Jewish, but he was still more vague about why anyone would want to make something of that. This bully liked to flick people's ears with his middle finger, shooting it off his thumb. When he tried it this time, Driver met his wrist halfway with one hand, stopping it cold. With the other hand he reached across and very carefully broke the boy's thumb.

The other thing Herb did, was race cars at a track out in the desert between Tucson and Phoenix, in this truly weird landscape inhabited by ten-foot-high dust devils, cholla that looked like some kind of undersea plant gone astray, and grand saguaro cacti with limbs pointing to heaven like the fingers of people in old religious paintings, riddled with holes hosting generations of birds. The track had been built by a group of young hispanics who, rumor had it, controlled the marijuana traffic up from Nogales. Herb was an outsider, but welcome for his skills as driver and mechanic.

First few times Driver went along, Herb would send him out to run the track with cars he'd just worked up, wanting to watch their performance. But once he got a taste of it, Driver couldn't hold himself back. He started pushing the cars, giving them their head, seeing what was in there. Soon it became clear he was a natural. Herb stopped driving and stayed in the pit after that. He tore the cars down and put them back together, same thing you do to build muscle; Driver took them out into the world.

It was also at the track that Driver met his only other good friend, Jorge. Just beginning to find the one thing he would ever be good at, Driver was astonished at someone like Jorge, who seemed so effortlessly good at everything. Played guitar and accordion in a local conjunto and wrote his own songs, drove competitively, was an honor student, sang solos in the church choir, worked with troubled juveniles at a shelter. If the boy owned a shirt besides the one he wore to church, Driver never saw it. He was always in one of those old-style ribbed undershirts, black jeans and gray nubbly cowboy boots. Jorge lived in South Tucson, in a shambling, much-amended house with three or four generations of family and an indeterminate number of children. Driver'd sit there chowing down on homemade tortillas, refried beans, burritos and pork stew with tomatillos surrounded by people babbling away in a language he couldn't understand. But he was a friend of Jorge's so he was family too, no question about it. Jorge's ancient abuela was always the first to rush out onto the dirt driveway to greet him. She'd ferry him in, forearm clamped against hers as though they strolled the boardwalk, babbling away excitedly the whole time. Out back often as not there'd be drunken men with guitarrons, guitars and mandolins, violins, accordions, trumpets, the occasional tuba.

That's where he learned about guns, too. Late evening, the men would get together and head out into the desert for target practice, both *practice* and *target* pretty much euphemism. Sipping at six packs of beer and bottles of Buchanan's scotch, they blazed away at anything in sight. But for all their seeming carelessness over application, they took the instruments dead seriously. From them Driver learned how these small machines must be respected, how they had to be cleaned and set up, why certain handguns were preferred, their quirks and shortcomings. Some of the younger men were into other things, like knives, boxing and martial arts. Driver, always a watcher and a quick study, picked up a few things from them as well, just as, years later, he'd pick things up from stunt men and fighters in movies he worked on.

Chapter Thirty-one

He took Nino down at six a.m. on a Monday. Weather report said it would climb to a balmy 82-degree high, gentle clouds from the east, forty percent chance of light rain later in the week. In slippers and a thin seersucker bathrobe Isaiah Paolozzi came out the front door of his Brentwood home, his mission twofold. Pick up this morning's *L.A. Times* from the drive. Fire up the sprinklers. Never mind that each burst from those sprinklers was water stolen from others. No other way you turned a desert into sculptured green lawns.

Never mind that Nino's entire life was stolen from others.

As Nino bent to pick up the paper, Driver stepped out of the recess beside the front door. He was there when Nino turned.

Eye to eye, neither blinked.

"I know you?"

"We spoke once," Driver said.

"Yeah? What'd we talk about?"

"Things that matter. Like how once a man makes a deal he keeps to it."

"Sorry. Don't remember you."

"What a surprise."

Perfect round hole between his eyes, Nino staggered back against the partially opened front door, pushing it the rest of the way open. His legs remained on the porch. Varicose veins like thick blue snakes stood out on them. A slipper fell off. His toenails were thick as planks.

From somewhere back inside the house, a radio issued morning traffic reports.

Driver set the box with its large pepperoni, double cheese, no anchovies, on Nino's chest.

The pizza smelled good.

Nino didn't.

Chapter Thirty-two

It looked just as he remembered.

There are all these places in the world, he thought, all these pockets of existence, where nothing much ever changes. Tide pools.

Amazing.

Mr. Smith, he assumed, was off at work, the Mrs. at one or another of her endless meetings. Church, school board, local charities.

He pulled up in front of the house.

Neighbors would be peeking out their windows, fingering slats of venetian blinds apart, wondering what business anyone driving a classic Stingray could possibly have with the Smiths.

What they saw was a young man climbing from the car, going around to the passenger side to extract a new cat carrier and a well-worn duffel bag. On the porch he set these down. He stepped close to the door, after a moment eased it open. They watched him pick up the cat carrier and duffel bag and step inside. Almost immediately he was walking back down the drive. He got in the Corvette and drove away.

He remembered how it had been, everyone knowing everyone else's business, all the open secrets, the lot of them believing they had the only true, real life and all others were counterfeit.

Along with the cat carrier and duffel bag he'd left a note.

> *Her name is Miss Dickinson. I can't say she belonged to a friend of mine who just died, since cats don't belong to anyone, but the two of them walked the same hard path, side by side, for a long time. She deserves to spend the last years of her life in some security. So do you. Please take care of Miss Dickinson, just as you did me, and please accept this money in the spirit it's offered. I always felt bad about taking your car when I left. Never doubt that I appreciate what you did for me.*

Chapter Thirty-three

Couldn't have been easy for his father. Driver didn't remember much about it, really, but even then, as a kid, dawn of the world, he'd known things weren't right. She'd put eggs she forgot to hard-boil on the table, open cans of spaghetti and sardines and throw them together, serve up a platter of mayonnaise and onion sandwiches. For a time she'd been obsessed by insects. Whenever she found one crawling, she'd cover it with a water glass and leave it to die. Then (in his father's words) she "took up with" a spider that established a web in one corner of the tiny half-bath where she retired each morning to apply the eyeliner, foundation, blush and cover providing the mask without which she would not launch herself into the world. She'd catch flies in her hand and throw them onto the web, prowl outside at night for crickets and moths and deliver those. First thing she'd do upon return, any time she left the apartment, was check on Fred. The spider even had a name.

Mostly, when she spoke to him at all, she just called him boy. Need any help with schoolwork, boy? Got enough clothes, boy? You like those little cans of tuna for lunch, right, boy? and crackers?

Never close to the ground, she drifted ever farther away from it, until he began to think of her as somehow *exempt*, not so much above this world as several steps to one side or the other of it.

Then that night at dinner with the old man spewing blood onto his plate. Ear there too, like a portion of meat. Driver's sandwich of Spam and mint jelly on toast. As his mother so carefully set down butcher and bread knives, perfectly aligned, having no further need of them.

I'm sorry, son.

Could this be a real memory? And if so, why had it taken so long to emerge? Could his mother actually have said that? Spoken to him that way?

Imagination or memory, let it go on.

Please.

Probably I've only made your life more complicated. Not what I'd hoped for....Things get so tangled up.

"I'll be okay. What's going to happen to you, Mom?"

Nothing that hasn't already. Time to come, you'll understand.

Imagination. He's pretty sure of that.

But now he finds himself wanting to tell her how, as time has gone by, he *doesn't* understand.

How he never will.

Meanwhile he'd ridden his new buggy home to the latest of local habitations. Name: Blue Flamingo Motel. Weekly rates, nothing much else around and a generous expanse of parking lot, ready access to major arteries and interstates.

Settling in, he poured half a fist of Buchanan's. Traffic sounds, TV from rooms close by. Spin, bang, slide and clatter of skateboards out on the parking lot, a favorite with neighborhood kids, apparently. Thwack of the occasional traffic or police helicopter overhead. Pipes banged in the walls whenever neighboring roomers roused and took to showers or toilets.

He picked up the phone on the first ring.

"I hear it's done," his caller said.

"Done as it'll get."

"His family?"

"All still asleep."

"Yeah. Well, Nino never slept much himself. I told him it was a bad conscience working its bony fingers up into him. He claimed he didn't have one."

A moment's silence.

"You didn't ask how I knew where you were."

"Tape across the bottom of the door. You replaced it, but it never quite re-adheres."

"So you knew I'd be calling."

"Sooner rather than later, I assumed—given the circumstances."

"Kind of pitiful, aren't we, the two of us? All this high technology swarming about us and here we are still relying on a piece of Scotch tape."

"One tool's much like another, long as it gets the job done."

"Yeah, I know something about that. Been something of a tool myself, all my life."

Driver said nothing.

"Fuck it. Your job's done, right? Nino's dead. What's left on the plate? You see any reason this should go on?"

"It doesn't have to."

"Got plans for tonight?"

"Nothing I can't ignore."

"Okay. So here's what I'm thinking. We get together, have a few drinks, maybe dinner after."

"We could do that, sure."

"You know Warszawa? Polish joint, corner of Santa Monica and Lincoln Boulevards?"

One of the ugliest streets in a city of many, many ugly streets.

"I can find it."

"Unless you insist on pizza."

"Funny."

"Yeah. It was, actually. All those coupons. Place—Warszawa, you got that, right?—shares its parking lot with a carpet store, but no problem, there's plenty of room. Around, what? Seven? Eight? What works for you?"

"Seven's good."

"It's a small place, no bar or anything like that where you can wait. I'll go on in, get us a table."

"Sounds good."

"Time we met."

Putting the phone to rest, Driver poured another couple of inches of Buchanan's. Close to noon now, he reckoned, most of the city's good folk itching to bail on job and duty and escape to lunch or a stamp-size park somewhere. Call home, see how the kids are, place a bet with the bookie, set up a meet with the mistress. The motel was deserted. When housekeeping knocked at the door, he said he was fine, didn't need service today.

He was remembering a time not long after he'd come to L.A. Many weeks of scrambling to stay off the streets, to stay out of harm's way and that of cruising sharks, scavengers and cops, scrambling just to stay alive, stay afloat. All was anxiety. Where would he live? How would he support himself? Would Arizona authorities suddenly appear to haul him back? He lived, slept and ate in the Galaxie, gaze ratcheting from street to roofs and windows nearby, back to the street, to the rear view mirror, to shadows back in the alley.

Then a great peace came over him.

He opened his eyes one day and there it was, waiting, miraculous. A balloon in his heart. He got his usual double hit of coffee at the mom-and-pop convenience store nearby, took up squatting space on a low wall before hedges entangled with food wrappers and plastic carry bags, and realized he'd been sitting there for almost an hour without ever thinking once about....well, anything.

This is what people are talking about when they use words like grace.

That moment, that morning, came vividly back to him whenever he thought of it. But soon suspicion set in. He understood well enough that life by very definition is upset, movement, agitation. Whatever counters or denies this can't be life, it has to be something else. Was he caught in some variant of that abstract, subatmospheric nonworld where his mother's life had simmered away unnoticed? Luckily, this was about the time he met Manny Gilden.

And now, from a phone booth outside the mom-and-pop convenience store, just as he did that long-ago night, he calls Manny. Half an hour later they're walking by the sea out Santa Monica way, a stone's throw from Warszawa.

"Back when we first met," Driver said, "and I was just a kid—"

"Looked in a mirror lately? You're still just a fuckin' kid."

"—I told you how I was at peace, how it scared me. You remember that?"

A museum of American culture in miniature, a disemboweled time capsule—burger and taco sacks, soda and beer cans, tied-off condoms, magazine pages, articles of clothing—washed up on shore with each thrust of the waves.

"I remember. What you'll find out is, only the lucky ones are able to forget."

"Sounds heavy."

"Line from a script I'm working on."

Neither spoke for a while then. They walked along the beach, this whole other demotic, bustling life, one they'd never know or be a part of, encircling them. Skaters, muscle men and mimes, armies of carefree young variably pierced and tattooed, beautiful women. Manny's latest project was about the Holocaust and he was thinking of Paul Celan: *There was earth inside them, and they dug.* These people seemed somehow to have dug free.

"I told you my story about Borges and Don Quixote," he said to Driver. "Borges is writing about that great sense of adventure, of the Don's riding out to save the world—"

"Even if it's only a few windmills."

"—and some pigs.

"Then he says: 'The world, unfortunately, is real; I, unfortunately, am Borges.'"

They'd come back around, to the parking lot. Manny walked to a forest-green Porsche and unlocked it.

"You've got a Porsche?" Driver said. Christ, he didn't even think Manny drove. Way he lived, way he dressed. Asking if Driver could take him to New York.

"Why'd you call, boy? What did you want from me?"

"The company of a friend, I think."

"Always a cheap treat."

"And to tell you—"

"That you're Borges." Manny laughed. "Of course you are, you dumb shit. That's the whole point."

"Yes. But now I understand."

Chapter Thirty-four

The carpet store was doing good business.

Not that Warszawa was exactly slouching.

It was a typical 1920s bungalow, Craftsman probably, rooms opening into one another with no halls. Hardwood floors, large, double-hung windows. Three rooms had become dining areas. The largest was divided by a half-wall. In the next, French doors opened onto a brick walkway planted with morning glories. In the third, smallest room a family party was underway. Squarish people looking much alike kept arriving with stacks of wrapped packages.

Lace curtains framed open windows. No air conditioning or need for same here so close to water's edge.

Bernie Rose sat at a corner table in the second room by the French doors with three-quarters of a bottle and half a glass of wine before him. The older man rose as Driver approached and put out a hand. They shook.

Dark suit, gray dress shirt with cufflinks buttoned to the top, no tie.

"Care for a glass, to start with?" Rose said as they sat. "Or would you prefer your usual scotch?"

"Wine's good."

"Actually, it is. Amazing what's out there these days. Chilean, Australian. This one's from one of the new Northwest vineyards."

Bernie Rose poured. They clinked glasses.

"Thanks for coming."

Driver nodded. An attractive older woman wearing a black miniskirt, silver jewelry and no stockings emerged from the kitchen and began moving table to table. Strains of Spanish that leaked through the kitchen door behind her caught a foothold. Driver still heard them as his companion went on.

"The owner," Bernie Rose said. "Never have known her name, though I've been coming here close to twenty years. Maybe she doesn't look *quite* as good in the outfit as she did back then, but...."

What she looked, Driver thought, was completely comfortable with herself, a quality uncommon enough anywhere, and one so remarkable in trendy, self-reinventive L.A., as to appear truly subversive.

"I can recommend the duck. Hell, I can recommend everything. Hunter's stew with homemade sausage, red cabbage, onions and beef. Pierogi, stuffed cabbage, beef roulades, potato pancakes. And the best borscht

in town—served cold when it's hot outside, hot when
a chill comes on. But the duck's to die for."

"Duck," Bernie Rose said when a college-age waitress with varicose veins, Valerie, came to the table, "and
another of these."

"The Cabernet-Merlot blend, right?"

"You got it."

"Duck," Driver echoed. Had he ever in his life eaten
duck?

Further squarish people with square wrapped packages arrived to be ushered into the third room. How
were they packing them all in? The owner came by in
her black miniskirt to hope they had a good meal and
to ask if they'd please let her know personally should
there be anything else they needed, anything she could
do for them.

Bernie Rose replenished glasses.

"You've been on a roll, boy," he said. "Cut yourself
quite a swath out there."

"I never asked for any of it."

"We usually don't. But it comes down on our heads
regardless. Thing that matters is what you do with it."
Looking off at the other diners, he sipped his wine.
"Their lives are a mystery to me, you know. Absolutely
impenetrable."

Driver nodded.

"Izzy and I've been together since before I can
remember. Grew up together."

"I'm sorry."

"Don't be."

Tasting the duck, he wasn't.

They knoshed down, dipped into the frosty pitcher of lemon-studded tea Valerie had set alongside.

"So where do you go from here?" Bernie Rose said.

"Hard to say. Back to my old life, maybe. If I haven't burned far too many bridges for that. You?"

He shrugged. "Back east, I'm thinking. Never much liked it out here anyway."

"Friend of mine claims the story of America is all about the advancing frontier. Push through to the end of it, he says, which is what we've done here at land's end, there's nothing left, the worm starts eating its own tail."

"Should have had the duck instead."

Despite himself, Driver laughed.

Working their way through a second bottle of Cabernet-Merlot and the second inning of this expansive meal, ordinary life going on about them, they'd landed for the moment on a kind of island where they might pretend to be a part of it.

"Think we choose our lives?" Bernie Rose said as they cruised into coffee and cognac.

"No. But I don't think they're thrust upon us, either. What it feels like to me is, they're forever seeping up under our feet."

Bernie Rose nodded. "First time I heard about you, word was that you drove, that's all you did."

"True at the time. Times change."

"Even if we don't."

Valerie brought the check, which Bernie Rose insisted upon paying. They walked out onto the parking lot. Stars bright in the sky. The carpet store was closing, families packing themselves into a fleet of battered trucks, decrepit Chevys, rip-off Hondas.

"Where's your ride?"

"Over here," Driver said. At the back edge of the lot, half hidden by a fenced area for garbage. Of course. "You don't think we change, then."

"Change? No. What we do is adapt. Get by. Time you're ten, twelve years old, it's pretty much set in you, what you're going to be like, what your life's going to be. *That's* your ride?"

A Nineties Datsun, much battered and devoid of a number of parts such as bumpers and door handles, piebald with rustoleum and filler.

"I know, it doesn't look like much. But then, neither do we. A friend of mine specializes in redoing these. Good cars to start with. When he finishes with them, they scream."

"Another driver?"

"Used to be, till both hips got shattered in a crash. That's when he started tearing them down, building them back up."

The parking lot was empty now.

Bernie Rose stuck out his hand. "Guess we won't be seeing one another again. Take care, boy."

Reaching to shake, Driver saw the knife—caught the flash of moonlight on it, actually—as Bernie Rose brought it out, left-handed, in a low arc.

He drove his knee hard against Bernie Rose's arm, caught his wrist as it shot up, and sank the knife into his throat. He'd struck a bit central, away from the carotids and other major vessels, so it took a while, but he'd taken out the pharynx and breached the trachea, through which Bernie Rose's last breaths whistled. So not too long.

Looking into Bernie Rose's failing eyes, he thought: This is what people mean when they use words like grace.

He drove the rest of the way down to the pier, bore Bernie's body to the edge of water and released it. From water we come. To water we return. The tide was going out. It lifted the body, carried it ever so gently away. City lights spackled the water.

Afterwards Driver sat feeling the fine roar and throb of the Datsun around him.

He drove. That was what he did. What he'd always do.

Letting out the clutch, he pulled from beach parking onto the street, reentering the world here at its very edge, engine a purr beneath him, yellow moon above, hundreds upon hundreds of miles to go.

Far from the end for Driver, this. In years to come, years before he went down at three a.m. on a clear, cool morning in a Tijuana bar, years before Manny Gilden turned his life into a movie, there'd be other killings, other bodies.

Bernie Rose was the only one he ever mourned.